Merry Kissmas

PIPER RAYNE

Cover Design and Illustrator: By Hang Le

1st Line Editor: Joy Editing

2nd Line Editor: My Brother's Editor

Proofreader: My Brother's Editor

About Merry Kissmas

Six years ago, he was her one-night stand, and now they're sharing a villa for the holidays.

I thought I was over him. That his good looks and British accent couldn't affect me anymore. But the minute our eyes lock across the elevator, all those feelings come roaring back to life.

Then I find out we're competing for the same job.

Next comes the realization that we have to spend a week together on a ski vacation because of some six-degree-of-separation nonsense.

The real kicker is when I find out the two of us have to share a villa. A very small, very cozy villa.

Needless to say, this Christmas getaway is starting off rockier than the mountains we'll be skiing down.

I've stayed away for years, what's one week? But I forgot how much easier it is to ignore him with an ocean separating us—especially when he's determined to win me back.

Merry Kissmas

Chapter One

BRYNN

I'm not off the plane and in the taxi for more than a minute when my watch vibrates.

Mom.

I should've known. Ever since my siblings and I agreed to give her the ability to track us as an early Christmas gift, she's been texting or calling whenever I've hit a pit stop on my journey from Portland to New York City.

I send her to voicemail and dig my phone out of my purse to send her a quick text.

> Hey, I'm in the taxi. Will call you when I get to the hotel.

> Just wanted to wish you good luck on the job interview!

> Thanks.

> Can't wait to see you. The snow makes for great skiing here. Your snowboard made it safe and sound.

My thumbs hover over the phone. I love my mom, but this is her way of finding out if I'm still upset about spending Christmas in a mountain resort town in Utah instead of my childhood home outside Portland, Oregon. My older brother, Tre, and his wife, Tessa, were the ones to bring up this winter escape to Utah. There was a family vote in October, and needless to say, I was the single one who voted to stay home.

Who cares about a lifetime of traditions? None of my family obviously.

> Can't wait to hit the slopes.

The three dots appear immediately.

> Love you. Remember, they'd be lucky to get you.

> Me: Thanks. Love you too.

I tuck my phone inside my purse and sit back in the taxi, admiring Christmastime in New York City. It doesn't come close to comparing to my small hometown of Climax Cove, but I chalk up my comparison to the sourness I feel about not getting my way.

That damn expectation from being the baby of the family popping back up.

The city glitters under the glow of colorful holiday lights. Strands of garland and wreaths hang on storefronts as shoppers bundled in heavy coats and wool hats hustle in and out with handfuls of shopping bags.

I jerk forward in my seat when the cab stops at a red light. The driver is busy honking his horn, yelling at the guy in front of him, while I admire the windows of a department store alive with animated dancing ballerinas.

There's a pulse to the season here, even in the gridlock of

traffic, that isn't present in Climax Cove. The city is alive, exciting, and electric. The holidays are everywhere you look.

But I'm not sure I can see myself living here.

There's a reason I decided to take a position with a marketing firm in Portland after college. I want to be close to my family, and New York City is about as far away as I can get. Sure, I have one brother, Carter, here, but everyone else is out west, and I love Oregon so much.

That said, there's also no way I was going to pass up an interview to be a marketing director with one of the biggest advertising firms in New York City. Who would have thought Enzo Mancini would call me, a twenty-five-year-old fresh face in the industry, off a referral from a mutual client? Not me.

The cab stops beside the curb in front of the hotel. I pay with my phone then step out, grabbing my suitcase and thanking the doorman when he opens the door.

The luxurious hotel lobby has been decorated with an elaborate array of twinkle lights, red bows, and more poinsettias than I've ever seen in one place in my life. Holiday music rings out, and a Christmas tree with fake snow on each branch and matching ornaments in red and green sits right in the middle.

I roll my suitcase over the marble floor, heading to the reception area to check in. After the attendant there gives me my room keys, I follow his instructions to the bank of elevators and press the up arrow.

More people join me in waiting while others walk past, and soon, I feel crowded in the small space like a herd of cattle at feeding time. The elevator dings, the doors open, and a rush of people file out before I'm shoulder-to-shoulder with strangers, moving toward the open doors and vying for a spot.

"What floor is everyone?" a man with a British accent asks, but I can't see his face because a guy I have to assume is a professional basketball player stands in front of me.

"Fifteen please," I squeak out.

"Done," he says.

Other people call out their floors, and I say a small prayer on our way up that we aren't over the weight limit. I'm not claustrophobic or scared of elevators, but the words death and trap come to mind.

The elevator stops at every single floor, and finally the man who might be taller than the Christmas tree in the lobby exits. I inhale a deep breath after being stuck in the corner. But the problem is, when I look around at who is left, the first person I get an eyeful of is the British man who took up the impromptu job of elevator operator. He's leaning with his back against the wall, ankles crossed, his head buried in his phone.

I freeze for a split second, and the air all rushes out of my lungs because I know exactly who he is.

I look left and right, as if I can escape before he sees me, but it's not a scene from *Mission Impossible.* Although I don't consider myself completely risk averse, I'm not up for the whole "opening the hatch to the elevator and climbing out the top" thing. As I'm about to turn around to give him my back, hoping he gets off on a floor before me, the elevator stops, and he glances up to check which floor we've stopped on.

Our eyes meet, and the affable look on his face transforms into shock first, confusion second, and finally settles on wariness.

I lift my hand and wave like an idiot, but hello, surprises make me antsy, especially the bad kind.

W hy my cousin loves this city, I have no clue. He should have stayed in London with me. With the way people push and crowd onto the elevator, you'd think the world is ending, and this thing is going to teleport us all to safety. And when did people stop having manners and common courtesy?

Of course, I get a spot right by the elevator buttons and have to chance getting everyone's winter cold by pressing every number from two to sixty.

As I wait for my floor, I don't want to engage in conversation, so I bury my head in my phone as if I'm someone important who can't spend a minute on an elevator without someone demanding my time.

The fine hairs rise along the back of my neck, and I get the distinct sensation that someone is staring at me. The elevator dings, giving me an excuse to look up, and bloody hell, I can't believe who's looking back at me. It can't be her.

Yet I know it is.

Long dark hair, brown eyes that drew me in all those years ago at the pub where we first met. I've thought of her too

5

many times to count over the years. She's gorgeous now, whereas I would have described her as cute and adorable back then.

Brynn lifts her hand up warily as if she thinks I've forgotten her. Never.

The doors shut, and the elevator lifts, along with my stomach.

All these years between us, and now she's standing in front of me.

I'm not a man accustomed to losing his ability to speak. Hell, I'm a professor, or at least I *was* a professor, of marketing.

"Hello, Brynn." I pocket my phone and step closer.

She steps back.

So, she still hates me. Got it.

"Hello, Mr....Pierce."

I chuckle because that was our exact problem, wasn't it? Who exactly was I to her? Not who I wanted to be, that's for sure, but there was a lot riding on my future when we first met.

"How have you been?" I ask.

That's the best I can do? I sound like a complete prat.

I really hate the judgmental arse who lives inside my head.

"Good."

Brynn looks next to her, where a petite woman is staring between the two of us, watching our interaction. Her smile is wide and welcoming as if we're a show, and she won first row seats.

"You?" Brynn asks, looking away from the woman.

"Good."

So, we're both good. That's good.

"What are you..." she asks at the same time I ask, "Do you live here?"

You knob. Why would she be at a hotel with luggage if she lived here?

"My cousin lives here," I answer first, with the hopes she'll forget what I asked her.

"Nice. No, I'm here for...well, I don't live here."

So, she's being dodgy about why she's here. Interesting. I didn't speak all my truth either, so I can't fault her.

"Fifteen!" a man calls when the elevator stops and the doors start to open.

Brynn smiles. The same one she'd give me in front of Professor Jorgensen. There's not one genuine muscle working in her face right now.

"It was nice seeing you. Enjoy your holiday." She wheels out her suitcase.

I almost don't get off because I don't want to seem stalkerish. But my room is on this floor, and it's absurd that I'm worried what she'll think when we'll likely go another six years without seeing one another again.

"Actually, this is my floor too." I step out, the doors shutting behind me.

"Oh, well..." She looks at the signs for which direction to head for her room. "I'm this way."

"Me too," I say, shaking my head, following her.

"This is getting weird." She stops so abruptly I almost trip over her suitcase but catch myself. "What room are you in?"

"Fifteen-thirty-one."

She pulls out her keycard envelope, and her jaw opens when she holds it up at me. "Fifteen-thirty-three."

Meaning we're sharing a wall. How wonderful. I get to spend the night thinking about how she's only feet away from me. This year keeps giving over and over again.

I'm not sure what to say before we part, but that arse inside my head speaks up before I can stop him. "Want to get a drink?"

She's quiet, and the regret of asking sinks deeper into my skin as if it's a toxin that's making my temperature rise.

"Sorry, I'm super tired from my flight. But I'm sure with that accent of yours, you'll find someone to join you in no time." She turns and aggressively tugs her suitcase down the hall.

I follow her. "Not everyone loves a British accent."

She stops at her door, and I stop at mine, then our eyes lock. "Let's not pretend I'm the only American girl you've had in your bed."

"You're not the only one, but you were the best."

She huffs, and her eyes, perfectly lined with a dark eyeliner, narrow. "And here I thought maybe you'd changed. Lost that cocky attitude of yours."

"On the contrary, I'm paying you a compliment, not myself." I pull out my keycard, and she raises hers, both of our cards hovering just above the locks.

"Well, it wasn't what happened in the bed that you needed to work on. It was what happened afterward where you fell short."

How have we possibly just gone from shock, to cordial, to throwing insults.

"I see you're still as immature as a teenage girl."

She scoffs as if I can't make a dig at her. "Sorry I wasn't one of the groupies following you around campus. I had higher goals than being your Wednesday night girl."

I shake my head, frustration mounting because she'll never understand that what happened with us wasn't all under my control. "Bloody hell, I was your TA. What did you want me to do?"

Are we really going to have this knockdown, drag-out fight in the hallway of a hotel?

"Treat me like I wasn't just some girl who landed in your bed that you could just toss to the side. I was just as shocked as you when I got into that classroom," she whisper-shouts as if we're back at the university with ears all around.

"It was my first year, I was trying to make a good impression. The fact that I slept with a student wasn't going to win me any brownie points with the professor. There are rules in place." The anger and frustration I felt then that my hands were tied, that there wasn't anything I could do about my feelings for Brynn, rises to the surface. Especially because I felt something I hadn't felt with any other woman prior.

"It was a conversation, Pierce. I never asked you to sleep with me in secret." She scans her keycard, and I want to rip it out of her grip, not let her step into that room and disappear from my life again. She twists the doorknob, and my stomach sinks.

"Let me buy you a drink," I blurt like a bumbling fool.

Her laugh echoes through the hallway. "Funny, that's what you said to me the first time we met. But I'm not as foolish as you seem to assume, and I don't repeat my mistakes. Happy holidays, Pierce. I do hope Santa brings you some coal for your stocking." Her smile is sarcastic, and she walks into her room, the door slamming behind her.

Goddamn it. I slide my own keycard into the lock and disappear into my room.

This is not what I need the night before the most important interview of my life.

I ditch my suitcase by the dresser and throw myself on the bed.

Seriously, universe? You pick right now to bring him back into my life?

I scramble to get up, grabbing my purse and digging for my phone. I need to talk to someone about what just happened.

Then I realize, I never told anyone about Pierce. And I don't feel like going into the embarrassing story about how little Brynn was a foolish girl thinking one weekend spent with a guy she met in a different country was some form of kismet.

I shake my head at that version of me's idiotic idea that the first guy she picked up at a pub was somehow waiting his entire life for her to walk through the door. As if there was a warm yellow glow lit behind her.

So naive.

So stupid.

So delusional.

But seeing him again stirs up all those feelings. His tall, lean, yet muscular frame still holds an air of confidence that he's comfortable with himself. The way his eyebrows pinch together when he's thinking about something. His stupid defined jawline and strong nose. He's damn perfection, and even though it's been years, the sight of him makes me draw a shallow breath.

A drink? Is he crazy? Hell no.

I lie back down and stare at the ceiling, my mind unable to avoid going back to the moment I've pushed away for years. Talk about Christmas magic, there was something in the air that night.

I had arrived in London three days before and was all settled in my dorm room. My mom wasn't thrilled with me studying abroad for the semester. Especially with my brother in the military. I'd witnessed the fear for his safety keeping her up at night when my brother decided to join the army after high school. I didn't want to add more worry to her shoulders, but it was only for a semester. Of course, because my mom is awesome, she told me I could do it on the stipulation that if she called, I had one hour to get back to her. So far, I'd talked to her three times that day.

My roommate, Molly, asked me to go out, and I almost skipped it because I hadn't expected the feeling of being homesick to sink in so fast. London was an entire world away from everything I knew, and I was already regretting my decision. But I finally accepted trying to put myself out there and make a life for myself for the next few months.

I figured I'd have a couple beers, make small talk, and go back to my dorm room. I didn't expect him.

I was at the bar getting a refill, since my dorm mate had insisted on buying my first beer. In truth, I smelled Pierce before I saw him. He was sitting to my right with his back to me, and his cologne was crisp and woodsy. I thought of my brothers and that maybe whatever cologne it was would be a good gift for the holidays.

His friend saw me first, eyed me, and I smiled politely, but I wasn't interested. I tried not to pay attention, holding my money out for the bartender to come help me, but their conversation stalled next to me. When Pierce swiveled on his stool, it ran across my hip, and his knee ran along my outer thigh.

I glanced over, expecting to see a man, but not one so good-looking.

His emerald eyes challenged me to remember what I was doing moments before. It was his smile, though, the way it creeped up and up until his white teeth gleamed under his pink lips. He stole all my attention.

I knew he was older than me—that was evident in the way he didn't seem at all fazed that I was tongue-tied and unable to stop staring at him. In the quiet confidence that surrounded him.

"What can I get you?" the bartender asked with impatience in his tone.

I turned to look, and he was nodding like "get on with it."

"Oh...um...a beer."

"Which one?" the bartender asked, looking down the line at the rest of the people he needed to serve.

"Um...that one." I pointed at one of the beer pulls, hoping it wasn't a dark beer.

"Pint or half?" The bartender blew out a breath and shared an annoyed expression with Pierce.

I felt my cheeks heating up and suddenly wanted to start my trek back to Oregon even if I had to swim across the Atlantic to get there. "Which one is smaller?"

The bartender looked again—this time at Pierce's friend—and his shoulders slumped.

"May I?" Pierce asked me, his mesmerizing smile on display.

I nodded, unsure what to do.

"A pint of pale ale," Pierce said.

The bartender nodded and started to pour my beer.

"Thank you," I said.

"Tourist?" he asked, then leaned over and reached in his back pocket for his wallet.

"Kind of."

The bartender interrupted us. Had he not, maybe I would have told Pierce I was there for school, and we would have discovered who each of us were to the other and that would have been that.

"Let me buy you a drink," Pierce said, and the bartender disregarded my money and took Pierce's.

I roll my eyes at the memory of being in the pub that night. Getting up, I grab my suitcase and unpack, pushing all thoughts of Pierce away from me. It was a momentary blip. I won't see him again, and that will be the end of that.

My phone dings. I stop hanging up my clothes and answer the text in my family's group chat, which is always out of control, but even more so with Christmas almost right upon us.

> Tre: Still sour grapes about having to come here?

Attached is a picture of the inside of his cottage, complete with a roaring fireplace and Tessa sitting on the couch.

Mom chimes in immediately because I think her phone is glued to her hand until we're all there safe and sound, together again.

> Mom: Don't get her all riled up before the interview.

> Dad: She'll be fine. She's my rockstar. Everyone loves her winning personality.

> Carter: Winning personality? I thought I was your rockstar.

> Tre: Everyone knows I'm the rockstar. Hello, retired Army Ranger... I outrank both of you.

My thumbs hover over the screen because I'm not sure what to text. Pierce has my mind in a complete spin.

> Tessa: Ignore him, Brynn. You're going to have all the same comforts of being back home. Mom and I made sure of it.

> I'm tired from the flight. See you all tomorrow night. Which one of your sorry asses is picking me up?

Silence. Which is never a good sign with my family.

> Hello?

I feel as if they're all waiting for one of them to tell me some horrible news.

> Dad: It worked out well. Tessa's friends Kenzie and Andrew are coming in on the same flight as you, so you'll hitch a ride with them.

Okay, that's not bad at all, why would they be worried to tell me that?

> Cool.

I've met Kenzie and Andrew a handful of times, and they're always nice. The only problem is that Andrew is English, and every time I hear his accent, I'm reminded of the jackass on the other side of the wall. But I can't hate everyone in the entire country just because they share an accent with Pierce.

> Tre: Phew, that was easy.

> Why would I have a problem with that?

> Carter: Because you've been whining and complaining like you used to when we wouldn't let you tag along with us when you were a kid.

> Signing off now. Catch you guys tomorrow, or maybe I'll purposely miss my flight.

> Mom: Keep that tracker on.

> Dad: Stop it, boys.

> Tre: I didn't do anything.

> Tessa: You know Christmas isn't possible without you.

How did I score the nicest sister-in-law?

> Tessa: Plus, this one is waiting for her favorite auntie.

She sends a picture of my niece looking adorable in a Christmas onesie.

> Carter: Better hurry before she only wants me.

He sends a picture of my niece in his arms. Ryah is smiling with drool running down her chin.

> She'll always love me more. Just like Mom.

> Dad: Okay, putting a stop to this. You can all volley to be Mom's favorite when we're all here together. We can't wait to have you join us. I'd say good luck, but you don't need it. If they don't give you the job, then they're idiots.

> Thanks, Dad.

Everyone else sends messages like good luck and you got this. My family might give each other a lot of shit, but deep down, we all have each other's backs.

I change into my pajamas and am about to crawl into bed when I hear Pierce's door open and shut. I jog to the peephole, but I miss him. I don't care that he's probably on his way down to the bar to pick up some girl for the night. Nope.

Why would I care?

I don't.

But I do hope he gets coal in his stocking this year and drinks spoiled eggnog.

Chapter Four

BRYNN

I enter the high rise building that Mancini Advertising is in and go through security. Since my name is on the list, it's an easy process.

I'm wearing a black power suit that I scored from Nature's Edge six months ago. The same client who only uses Mancini Advertising for their ads but wanted a smaller marketing company to help with brand awareness.

On the elevator ride up to the top floor, I try to calm my nerves, reminding myself that Enzo Mancini called me, not the other way around. Plus, I'm not even sure I want to move to New York City. It'd be a drastic change from Portland, but at the same time, I'm young, and there's something about the idea of living in a city filled with millions of people before I have a husband and a family. I want them eventually, I'm just not sure when.

The elevator doors slide open, and I'm presented with the word Mancini in big chrome lettering on the wall across from me and a huge Christmas tree on either side. Each one is decorated with what looks like homemade ornaments and small stockings with the names of who I assume are the employees.

I read up on the company after I got the call. Enzo and his wife, Annie, built this place from the ground up. Taken themselves from millionaires to billionaires no doubt. The way he showcases his family on his about page, praising his wife for her genius ideas to get the company where it is today, says a lot about the man he is. At least in digital form, but I always trust my gut when I meet someone.

It's only steered me wrong once, and I chalk that up to a silly crush and a set of striking green eyes.

After the interview, I'll grab my luggage from the hotel, change, and go to the airport to fly to Utah to spend Christmas with my family in a villa instead of my childhood home. Hopefully, the bitterness will shake off me before I land.

I approach the reception desk with a smile. The man seated there looks up from his computer with a welcoming smile as if I'm his long-lost friend and we're being reunited. I know how he got his job.

"Welcome to Mancini Advertising. Brynn Russell, right?" He types on the keyboard and swivels back to look at me. "Mr. Mancini is just about done with his meeting before you. Can I get you a coffee or tea? Hot cocoa maybe? There are some homemade sugar cookies in the break room."

He rises to his feet. I wasn't expecting him to be so tall, and when I survey him, I notice that his pants are printed with Santas over a green fabric.

"Love the pants," I say, liking the vibe of this office. It seems casual and fun.

He glances down and laughs. "Thanks. It's our Christmas dinner tonight for the firm. My matching jacket is in the coat room."

"I imagine you'll be the best dressed one there."

"Oh no." He leans closer. "If you get hired, you'll have to up your game from this black ensemble you got going on. I mean, it's great for the interview, sharp and all. But we like bold around here."

I'm suddenly second-guessing my decision to dress in black. Maybe it's plain and boring. "I'll remember that. Thanks."

"So, can I get you something to drink while you wait?"

"No, thank you..." I realize I have no idea what his name is.

"Oh, sorry, Todd." Voices sound from down the hall, and Todd turns his head in their direction. "Looks like you won't be waiting long. And you get to see your competition." His eyebrows rise.

As they get closer, I hear their voices better, and what I hear has me stiffening. Because the one voice is English and sounds really damn familiar. I look in the direction of the voices and spot Pierce walking toward me with Enzo Mancini.

"Great to meet you," Pierce says, and my teeth grind together.

"I get that he's good-looking, but chill, girl," Todd whispers. "He's married."

"He is?" My head whips back in Todd's direction.

"Girl, you really should've done your research. Happily married, and she's probably going to be in the interview with him." He shoots me a "get a clue" look, and it dawns on me that he thinks I'm talking about Enzo.

"No, I was talking about the other guy."

Although Enzo has a hot dad vibe, it's the man in a suit that has to be tailor-made for his body that has my attention. His broad shoulders and taut waist... God, I need to stop envisioning my hands pulling at the belt buckle while his lips are on me, his hands in my hair. My stomach feels light in my body, as if it could float away.

"He's your competition. You want to sleep with the competition? I don't suggest it."

I watch the way Pierce interacts with Enzo, as though they're old drinking buddies swapping memories of their wild times together. Not like an interviewer and interviewee.

Pushing past all the lust threatening to take control of my brain and set me on a path that has nothing to do with my interview, I turn my attention back to Todd. "Do they know one another?"

Todd narrows his eyes a bit. "Why would he be here for an interview if they did?"

Okay, Todd, no need to be snarky, although he has a point.

The two men continue to talk, Enzo putting his hand out for Pierce to shake. Pierce's hand slides out of his pocket, not too eager, but not too lackadaisical either. He slips it into Enzo's hold without breaking eye contact. Is the man ever nervous? He has the same graceful ease he's always had. Just like the way he would stroll into the lecture hall and fold himself into the chair in the corner of the first row while Professor Jorgensen conducted his lecture.

"Go have a seat so it doesn't look like you just got here." Todd nudges my arm.

Good idea. I scramble to take a seat in the waiting area a few steps away, grabbing a magazine and holding it up in front of my face while I wait.

"Have a great trip. We'll be in touch after the holidays," Enzo tells Pierce.

"Oh no rush, enjoy your time with your family. Merry Christmas."

From behind my magazine, I stick my tongue out at Pierce for sounding so relaxed and unfazed.

Why is he interviewing for a job in New York when he's a professor in London? My gut twists with the knowledge that he has more experience than me. He's older and teaches marketing for shit's sake. But does he have life experience?

I bet not, *mate*.

I hear Todd and Enzo exchange words, but I'm too in my head about how Pierce probably just killed it in his interview to make sense of them.

A large hand lands on the spine of the magazine, startling me, and spins it around. "I don't recall seeing 'upside-down reader' on your resume."

It's Enzo. Enzo Mancini. And I look like a fool.

My cheeks heat, and my hands tremble slightly. I have nothing to say. Nothing to excuse why I would be pretending to read a magazine. Panic flares in my veins.

"I was just checking out the ads from a different angle." I inwardly sigh and wish there was a hole around here that could swallow me up.

He hums low in his throat. "Interesting. Enzo Mancini." He sticks out his hand in front of him. The same hand Pierce just touched.

Jesus, get him out of my head.

"Brynn. Brynn Russell, but you know that."

I hear Todd sigh as if I'm personally disappointing him. Maybe he sees the potential for our future lunches drifting away like I do.

"Good to meet you, Miss Russell."

We shake hands, and I try to be firm, but not too firm, and not weak either.

Enzo smiles, but his eyes dart in the direction over my shoulder. "Pierce, did you need something?"

So, I'm Miss Russell, but he's Pierce? I can already feel the favoritism.

"No," Pierce says.

I circle around and find him standing still without his usual confident air about him.

Surprise.

It's nice to see him a little off-kilter.

"I thought I forgot my cell phone." He pats the inside of

his suit jacket and retrieves it. "Got it. Have a Merry Christmas, and don't forget to send me a picture of that suit, Todd."

I shoot Todd a look accusing him of playing both sides, and he shrugs.

"I'll tag you."

"Be safe. Don't break anything." Enzo waves to Pierce.

Or do, I think, even though I have no idea where he's spending his holiday.

Pierce's gaze doesn't leave mine at first, but then it slides down my body and warmth spreads in its path. By the time his green irises meet my eyes again, I'm ready to drip into a puddle like a snowman under a heat lamp. God, how can he still have that effect on me after all this time?

"See you all after the holidays." Pierce lifts his arm with a wave and disappears toward the elevators.

I suck in a breath.

"Do you two know one another?" Enzo's question takes me out of my daze.

"Oh...um...no." I shake my head, but he tilts his head as if he's unsure I'm telling the truth.

"Well, let's get this interview going. I'm sure you're eager to start your holiday too." He steps back to allow me to exit the waiting area first. "I'm sorry this interview is so close to Christmas, but Annie and I didn't want to wait. We're hoping to kick off the new year having already made a decision. I'd also like to apologize that you had to see the other applicant. Usually, these things are more spaced out, but my schedule just didn't allow for it this week."

"No problem at all."

"There she is," Enzo says when a woman comes out of an office, walking down the hall.

I recognize her from their website. Annie Mancini. Her dark hair is cut into a bob, and her dress fits her perfectly, showing off an amazing figure.

It's the way the words come out of his mouth that causes me to turn away from her to look at him. His smile reaches his eyes, and it's the same way my brother Tre looks at Tessa. As if his world and all his happiness is wrapped up in her.

"Annie, this is Brynn Russell." Enzo makes the introductions and steps behind me to open a door.

I shake Annie's hand. "Nice to meet you."

"You too. Sorry, I was going to come and get you from the waiting area, but I got a phone call from the school." Her gaze flicks over my shoulder to her husband. "Our son Mateo just can't seem to stay in his seat."

"Or stop pranking," Enzo says as we file into the conference room.

"He learned it from his father and his uncles." She eyes him hard, and he puts his hands up in the air.

"I've apologized many times already."

We all take our seats.

"Did Todd offer you anything to drink?"

Enzo grabs an empty mug that I assume was Pierce's and sets it on the table by the wall.

"I'm okay, but thank you."

During the interview, they each have a way of putting me at ease, but all I can think about the whole time is that I'm going up against Pierce for this job. The competitive side of me that was born as the baby sister to two older brothers rises, and by the time it's over, I think I've done everything I can to show Enzo and Annie I'm the right one for the job.

I grin to myself when I'm leaving, and as the elevator doors slide closed, I anticipate the sweet taste of payback if I get the job over Pierce.

I sit in the back of the cab as a light sprinkling of snow starts to come down. I really hope it doesn't delay my flight. I don't hate Christmas, but it's not my favorite time of year either. It only serves as a reminder of what is missing in my life.

Which brings my thoughts back to Brynn. Not that she's been far from my mind since our meeting last night. And then again earlier today.

I see now why we were at the same hotel with rooms next to each other. The reservations for us were probably made at the same time when Mancini Advertising booked our trips for the interviews. I looked like an idiot when I ended my interview with Enzo Mancini and stood there slack-jawed, staring at Brynn. It wasn't my finest moment.

Of course, I knew there would be other interviewees, that I wasn't the only person Mancini Advertising had reached out to. News traveled fast after I left my professor position at the university. It would be nice to be close to my cousin again— I've missed him over the years. Which is one of the reasons why I said I would spend the holidays with him this year since I was already in America.

Brynn Russell.

There she is again, sneaking into my thoughts. She seems so different, but not at the same time.

As the snowflakes melt on the windshield, and I watch the people walking along the sidewalk, my mind goes back to that first night we met.

My mate noticed her first, and he still argues to this day that I stole her from him. He's probably right, but I don't care. She was worth the last six years of razzing from him, even if I only had her for such a short time.

She went so willingly to the table after I asked her to join me for a more private conversation.

Her infectious laugh, the way her body swayed closer to mine to hear me better after the pub got busier is still crystal clear in my memory, as is the ease and trust she had when I asked her to go for a walk and let me show her what I loved about London.

At first, we were walking six inches apart, but the distance shortened as the minutes turned to hours. When I finally took my hand out of my pocket and slipped it into hers with the excuse of guiding her away from a family coming toward us, she never said anything when I didn't release it.

She talked about her family, and for the first time in my life, I wasn't jealous someone else had it so good but, instead, glad that she had them since they clearly meant a lot to her.

It started to sprinkle, but we continued our walk. I'm pretty sure she didn't want the night to end as much as I did. When the rain really came down, I pulled her under the small awning of a store.

Our bodies were pressed together, and when she laughed, I

looked down at her, admiring her beauty. She was so damn beautiful, I didn't understand why she'd accepted my invitation in the first place. She was completely out of my league.

Her eyes locked with mine, and her laughter died. We were tucked away, sheltered from the sheets of rain coming down around us. I took my chance and lowered my head, hoping like hell I wasn't alone in this thing between us. I had never felt a connection with someone so quickly or so strong.

Her tongue slid across her lips, and I stopped an inch away.

"This okay?"

She nodded, fisting my jacket in both her hands, tugging me the rest of the way to her mouth.

I stepped into her, my hands cradling the sides of her head, my thumbs running along her cheeks. She slid her tongue into my mouth first, but I deepened our kiss while the thrill of exhilaration raced through my veins. Finally, I knew what she tasted like, and I only wanted more. It wasn't enough.

I pressed my body against hers and slid my thigh between her legs. She ground against me and reached around my neck, her fingers running through my hair and up the back of my head. The sound of the raindrops pattering to the ground fell into the background, replaced by the sounds of our heavy breathing and moans.

I stripped my mouth off hers, and my lips fell to her jaw. "Come home with me," I said in way too desperate of a voice.

Her body stiffened under my hands. "I..."

"Shit, I'm sorry." It took every ounce of my willpower to step away from her, giving her space. Why would she come home with me? She didn't even know me.

She stumbled forward from the abruptness of my movement but straightened quickly. "It's just, I don't...I mean, I don't know you and...I want to, though."

I took her declaration as an opening to maybe. I knew I was

a good guy, that she could trust me, but she didn't know that. Taking her hand, I flipped it palm up, dug into my pocket, and put my wallet in it. "Go ahead. Take a picture of my license, send it to your mum."

"We're not involving my mom in this." She giggled, then stared at the closed wallet.

I watched her tits rise and fall with her deep breaths. I waited, leaning against the brick wall across from her. I was antsy, and for the first time in a long time, I thought maybe I wasn't going to get what I wanted. That I'd be the polite guy, walk her home, and hopefully if I was lucky, we'd exchange numbers. Maybe I'd get the chance later on to woo her. I was willing to wait as long as she needed. I just didn't want that night to be the only time I saw her.

Her gaze floated up to mine, and the corners of her lips tipped into a smile I hadn't seen from her yet. She cupped my wallet and held it out for me to take back. "You should know that one of my brothers is an army ranger and can hunt you down while you're sleeping and cut off your balls."

Taking my chances, I stepped back into her space. "Noted."

She rose up on her tiptoes, but I snaked my arm around her waist, pulling her into me. My lips fell to hers because I needed another fix, and she met my tongue stroke for stroke.

She closed the kiss and drew back. "I thought you were taking me to your place."

"I want to, but I'm having a hard time stopping myself from kissing you."

She giggled and pressed her lips to mine. I looked lame in my attempt to keep on kissing her when she stepped out into the rain and onto the sidewalk. "Easy fix. You can't kiss me until I'm in your apartment."

The rain made her long chestnut strands darken and stick to the side of her face. She tipped her head back and closed her eyes, letting the droplets rain down on her face.

At that moment, I knew she was one of those people who might come in and out of my life but would never truly leave me. That I'd remember that moment until my dying breath.

I stepped out of the alcove and took her hand, flagging down a hackney.

Fifteen minutes later, I finally had her in my place, and I wasted no time pressing her back to the door and devouring her mouth once again.

The memory comes to an abrupt halt when the Uber parks along the curb at my cousin's brownstone. There's a wreath on not only the front door, but on every window, and it makes me think I have the wrong place. Garland is woven through the black wrought-iron railings that lead up to the door. And are those fake reindeer at the base of the stairs? As an adult, he's never been that into Christmas, especially after what happened to him all those years ago.

I step out, and the driver retrieves my suitcase from the boot.

Walking up the steps, I spot elf figurines on the other side of the door and the welcome mat reads "Merry Christmas from the Wainwrights" with their names on stockings. So I suppose I am in the right place.

I press the doorbell, and "All I Want for Christmas" by Mariah Carey plays.

How clever.

My cousin opens the door. "Pierce," he says with a smile.

Behind him, all I see are more Christmas decorations.

"Are you sure I'm at the right house? It looks like Christmas threw up around here."

He chuckles and steps aside, inviting me in. "Yeah, well… things change. Come in and tell me about the interview."

I wheel in my suitcase and leave it by the door. I can tell

one thing for sure—my cousin has built a home with his wife. I push aside the envy quickly taking me over so I might enjoy my time here rather than focusing on what I don't have. But damn it all to hell if Brynn hasn't made all that hope resurface.

Chapter Six

BRYNN

"Traveling on the last business day before the holidays, huh?" Butch, my Uber driver, is a chatty one when I just want to sit quietly and dissect how the interview went.

Annie was very pleasant and sweet. Enzo was too, but he asked me the more typical hard-hitting questions, whereas Annie's were more thought-provoking. The two of them were super professional, but it's clear they're a couple from the way they look at one another. Him especially. It's nice to see a man who adores his wife.

I'm not sure I'll ever find that, but then again, I'm still young.

"Yeah, I was only in town for a night."

"And where are you headin'?"

I usually don't mind talking to my drivers, but I just want to get to the airport, find my gate, and get on the plane, even if it's not where I want to go right now. What would my family do if I decided to rebook the flight Mancini Advertising booked for me and head to Portland? Although that would be lonely, since I'd spend Christmas by myself.

"Utah," I answer.

"Visiting family?"

He looks at me through the rearview mirror, and I smile. It's not genuine, but he probably doesn't see that. "Yep."

Finally, he turns off the main road to follow the airport signs. I collect my purse, ready to hop out, but he abruptly stops in a line of traffic.

"Busiest day for travel," he says, shaking his head.

I groan and throw myself back into the seat. Lifting my wrist, I check my watch to make sure I have time for this delay.

Inch by inch, we move forward while Christmas carols ring out of the stereo. Butch sings along to each one. I have a feeling—from the holiday lights around the inside of his car and the stuffed reindeer that's been fixed to the grill—that he's a Christmas lover. Normally I am too, but a little more subdued.

"I hope you have TSA pre-check. Security is going to be a nightmare," Butch says, his eyes finding mine in the rearview mirror once again. He's spent more time looking through that than the windshield.

"I do." I don't have to travel a lot, but enough that it makes it convenient for me.

We finally get closer to the actual airport, and I need to tip Butch extra because he snakes his way in and out of the line of cars, cutting people off, so that we move along faster than we would have.

"I'm not sure I can get you any closer," he says, four car lanes away from the curb.

"No problem. I'll get out here." I open the door and quickly climb out.

He meets me at the trunk, pulling out my bag and handing it to me. "Merry Christmas, Brynn. Enjoy your time with your family."

My shoulders slump because I'm really being a grinch this

holiday season. What's wrong with an Uber driver who wants to talk and sing carols? Absolutely nothing.

"Thank you, Butch. You too."

I tip him extra for the holidays, and because he didn't get the best version of me, and make my way safely to the curb.

Going through check-in and security is agony because even TSA pre-check is busy. Deciding to find my gate first, I realize I have hardly any time before we take off. The beautiful holiday decorations are lost in the sea of busy travelers hustling as if it's Black Friday, and they're out to score the latest door special.

I don't catch a lot of smiles. In fact, most people look annoyed or pissed off.

Finally, I reach my gate, and I completely forgot until now that Kenzie and Andrew will be on my flight. Shit, I'm not in the mood to socialize. And although I don't have to worry about Andrew on that front, Kenzie is a talker. Normally I enjoy it, but I'm mentally drained from the mix of a huge interview and having Pierce floating into my mind every time I have a quiet moment.

On second thought, Kenzie is perfect. She'll keep my mind on things that don't include hot English guys.

"Kenzie," I say, waving and breaking the distance to where she and Andrew sit by the window.

Andrew is leaning back, his legs crossed, reading a book, while Kenzie's head is buried in her phone with her head on Andrew's shoulder. I assume the stroller next to them has their little guy in it. They really are one of those couples single girls get jealous over. Kenzie found her one and only, but I'm still searching for mine.

She lifts her head and says something to Andrew to make him lower his book and follow her line of vision. "Hi, Brynn."

Kenzie is dressed in jeans and a T-shirt that reads, "I'm so Elfin' cute."

"Love the shirt," I say, stopping in front of them.

She stands and extends her arms. "Andrew's early gift to me," she says, looking down at it. "It's an inside joke."

I wrap my arms around her, and she squeezes me hard.

Once she releases me, Andrew sets his book on Kenzie's empty chair and hugs me. "Brynn, wonderful to see you again."

I politely hug him, but not nearly as tightly as I did Kenzie. When we all part, I take the seat across from them.

"Is Nolan sleeping?" I ask, pointing at the stroller.

"Yes, and if we're really lucky, he'll sleep through the flight." Kenzie crosses her fingers. "But he's pretty excited to see his girlfriend." She laughs, and Andrew rolls his eyes.

"Still trying to make sure they marry one another?" I giggle at the fact that Tessa and Kenzie have been swearing their children will marry one another someday whether they want to or not. There are only two months difference between them.

"Of course. And then we'll really be related." Kenzie's voice is so loud that a few people glance over.

"What brought you to New York City, Brynn? Kenzie never said," Andrew asks.

Her head whips in his direction. "Yes, I did, but your head has been buried in that book since the moment you bought it."

He shrugs and looks at me for an answer.

"Oh, I had a job interview."

"That's funny," he says and glances at Kenzie.

"Not really. There are how many businesses in New York City?" Kenzie laughs and playfully smacks Andrew's shoulder.

He nods. "True."

"What am I missing?" I ask, looking between the two of them.

"Andrew's cousin was in town for an interview too. People

must be trying to get them in before the holidays." Kenzie wiggles in her seat, crossing her legs.

"Definitely not ideal." I look at the board, and it says we're boarding in twenty minutes. "Can I leave my carry-on here? I'm just going to run and grab some gum and maybe find a book of my own."

Kenzie waves me off. "Yeah, I'm not chancing moving this kid until we're on the plane."

"Thanks so much." I stand and head to the closest store.

I weave through the throngs of people feeling like a salmon swimming upstream, and I'm about to step into the store when a big body darts in front of me.

"Oh, sorry." The crisp English accent is way too familiar, and my stomach clenches.

I lift my head, and sure enough, it's fucking Pierce.

"This is beyond coincidental at this point. Shouldn't you be in the international terminal?" I swivel to go around him, but he grabs my wrist, stopping me, causing a woman to huff and swear under her breath as she weaves around us.

"Wait," he says. "How did the interview go?"

I raise my eyebrows. "How did yours go?"

"I didn't know," he says as if I thought he did.

"Obviously."

He stares down at my wrist, his thumb running along the inside right before he drops it, and my arm falls to my side. "Listen."

I see it in his eyes—he's going to broach the subject when I really wish he'd leave it in the past. "It's okay. I know you're sorry."

"No," he says.

"You're not sorry?"

"No, I am. Of course I handled that entire situation like a complete prat, but I mean, I wondered if...I'm in America until after the new year and wondered if perhaps I could get your phone number. Before I return to London, I could fly to see you."

My eyes widen. "Why?"

A man in a business suit stares us down, and Pierce apologizes, grabbing my hand and guiding us next to the wall where we aren't in people's way. It's an effort to pretend that I don't like the feel of his skin against mine.

"You know why."

"I don't. It's been six years, Pierce. Why now?" I'm on social media. If he wanted to find me before now, he could have.

I know the answer, though, because it's the same with me. I tucked him in a box. For me, it was my time in London. He was a memory, a moment in time I'd always remember, but never willingly revisit.

"Seeing you again—"

I shake my head. "I'm not that same girl anymore. The girl from that night doesn't exist. So, I can give you my phone number, and you can come to Portland, but the version of me you're remembering doesn't exist anymore."

He huffs out a breath, and his green eyes meet mine, scouring for the truth of my words. "I'd like it anyway."

"Pierce..." I search the walls for a clock. Any excuse to get out of this conversation. "My plane is going to board soon, I have to get some gum and—"

"Give me your phone." He holds out his palm.

I tip my head back. Why is he making this so hard? But he doesn't lower his hand. I dig into my purse, enter my password into my phone, and hand it over to him, though reluctantly. I can always block him if he tries to reach out to me.

He thumbs around with it, then places it in my hand. "There. Maybe it's Christmas. Maybe it's the magic of the holidays, although I'm not big on them. Maybe we'll never be in contact, but I can't get on my plane knowing that I was too chickenshit to get your phone number. Somehow, knowing I'm only the press of a button away from hearing your voice calms me, even though neither of us may ever use it."

I put my phone back in my purse, trying to appear as unfazed as I can, but I know I'm losing the battle.

He leans forward before I can stop him, his lips to my cheek. "Merry Christmas, Brynn. I hope Santa brings you whatever you asked for."

Then he's gone.

Lost in the throng of people.

But I can still feel the ghost of his lips on my cheek.

I place my palm on the spot where he kissed me.

"Come on, lady, let's go," an older woman shouts from somewhere close to me.

I snap out of my fog and head in to buy some gum.

I'll never use that number, but at least this memory of Pierce is better than the last. The urge to call or text him rises up immediately, which is exactly why I'll be deleting his number when I get on the plane.

Chapter Seven

PIERCE

It's all George Michael's fault. Had he never written the song "Last Christmas" and had his band Wham! perform it, I wouldn't have heard it over the speakers in the airport store right before Brynn ran into me.

What is it about the holidays that make you relive life's decisions?

It seemed like fate that she was there right after I told myself that as soon as I was back from holiday, I'd look her up and try to get in contact with her.

I walk back to the gate, still in disbelief that she exchanged phone numbers with me. That has to be a good sign. One that would suggest she feels the same as me—that our time together might not be done.

I'm so lost in my thoughts that it takes me a moment to realize my cousin and his wife seem to be having a disagreement. The urge to turn around and head back into the store with Brynn rises, but that would be a little much. I don't want to push her too far, too fast.

"Hey," I say, my gaze falling to the suitcase sitting across from them. I'd swear it was Brynn's, but... "Where did this come from?"

Andrew looks at me. "It belongs to the woman I told you about."

"Woman?" He hasn't told me anything about a woman.

"You didn't bother telling him? Do you ever listen to me?" Kenzie picks up a crying Nolan out of the stroller and walks away, rocking him.

"I did." He pushes his hand through his hair. "Why is it always my fault?"

"Not that I'm taking sides, but you didn't tell me." I usually wouldn't ask questions about the suitcase or bother Andrew when he's clearly distracted, but it looks identical to the one Brynn wheeled down the hotel hallway last night.

He throws up his hands. "It's Kenzie's best friend's husband's sister. She's on our flight."

"Meaning she's joining us for the holidays?" My heart shouldn't soar with the thought that maybe it's Brynn.

Andrew stares long and hard at me, his expression suggesting he wants to punch me in the face if I ask one more question. "Since she's Tre's family, yes."

"Tre is the best friend's husband?" I ask, sitting down next to the suitcase. If it is Brynn's, I'll be waiting right here for her.

"Want me to map out a family tree?" His gaze follows Kenzie, who I assume is behind me somewhere. "Yeah, he's the husband."

"Does she live in New York?"

Andrew's gaze diverts to me, but only for a second before it returns to Kenzie.

"She has a crying baby, bloke. I don't think anyone is going to try and woo her away from you."

Now I earn his really pissed off look. The one I thought was only reserved for me when I beat him at Battleship.

"Well?" I ask.

"What?" He looks away from his wife and scowls at me.

"Does she live in New York?"

He shakes his head. "Here're all the details so that you can get off me about this. She was here for a job interview." He stops talking, and my heart picks up pace. Could it really be?

"Interesting..."

"So, she's going to get on the plane with us, and we're going to drive her to the mountain cabins we're staying in, where she'll be reunited with her brothers, her niece, her sister-in-law, and her parents. Is that enough information?" He stands—to walk toward Kenzie, I presume.

"What's her name?"

His shoulders slump, and he looks down at me. "Brynn."

He stalks toward Kenzie, and good thing because I'm at a loss for words. I reach for the tag on the abandoned luggage and flip it around to see Brynn Russell written there with a Portland address.

Holy shit. There's no possible way.

"Okay, who do you know at the airlines?" Brynn's voice rings out, and I swivel around to see her standing with a book in the crook of her arm, a bag of Skittles, a pack of gum, and a water. "And don't touch other people's suitcases."

She winds around me, pushes her suitcase with her feet, and sits one seat away from me. Choosing to sit next to some random guy who is consuming a burger as if he's been starved in a cage for the last week.

She must not know who I am to Andrew, and it pulls a satisfied grin out of me that I get to be the one to tell her.

"Why are you sitting at my gate, Pierce?" she asks, placing her purse on the seat between us and opening her Skittles.

"It's a funny story actually." I turn so I'm facing her.

Her dark eyebrows rise, but she looks bored with the game

43

I want to play with her. "What? You're going to Utah?" She rolls her eyes as though the idea is absurd.

"In fact, I am."

She tears the bag open too forcefully, and Skittles topple to the floor. "I'm sorry, what?"

All the kids nearby fall to their knees, picking up the candies. Their parents tell them to stop, but one little guy gets a handful into his mouth, and I cringe, watching him smile as his mum pulls him up off the floor.

"Oh god, I'm so sorry." Brynn abandons her half-full bag of Skittles and bends down to pick up the scattered colorful pieces.

I join her, both of us kneeling on the floor, scouring to find all the candies. I hope she knows I'd only do this for her.

She looks up at me with eyes full of shock and wariness.

"Oh good, you guys met. Why are you both on the floor picking up Skittles?" Kenzie says from behind me.

I stand, taking my handful of Skittles with me. Brynn does the same.

"I'm clearly missing something," Brynn says before walking to the trash can and tossing the Skittles inside.

I throw mine away too, and Kenzie grabs wipes from the diaper bag, handing them over to us. We both wipe our hands.

"Brynn, this is Andrew's cousin, Pierce. He's joining us on the trip," Kenzie says.

Brynn glares at me. "He's what? I didn't know anything about this."

Andrew, who is now holding Nolan, joins us, lowering his face closer to Kenzie's. "So, I'm not the only one who forgets to tell people things."

She narrows her eyes and disregards him. Andrew sits in his earlier seat.

"Oh great..." Brynn starts before anyone can say anything else. "So, first my family outvotes me and decides we're going to spend Christmas in some mountain town instead of the family home, then I run into my fling from London, find out he's my competition for my dream job, and now I have to spend the holidays with said fling." She throws her hands in the air. "Plus, my Skittles..." She looks longingly toward the trash can.

"Fling?" Kenzie asks. She turns to Andrew. "Did you know they knew each other?"

"Why would I know that?" he says.

Is this what a baby brings, testiness with one another?

Andrew and Kenzie stare at us, as does the burger-eating man and most everyone else around us. My gaze darts to Brynn. How much does she want to tell them?

"We're going to start the boarding process now..." one of the airline attendants at the gate announces.

"We'll catch up on the plane." Kenzie turns to Andrew, who is already swinging the diaper bag over his shoulder.

Andrew hands Nolan to Kenzie and breaks down the stroller. They work it like an assembly line, and not for the first time in my life, I'm impressed by my cousin.

"You'll understand when you have kids," Andrew says as he passes me.

The two of them walk toward the gate to wait to be the first to go in since they have a baby, leaving Brynn and me by ourselves.

"I cannot believe this." She puts her book in her purse and grabs the handle of her carry-on. "This is setting up to be my worst holiday ever."

"I think maybe it's a sign. We can use the time to reconnect." I take my small carry-on and swing it over my shoulder.

"We're not reconnecting." She barrels by me.

The burger guy gives me that look to say, "Sorry, mate, she's not interested."

And maybe she's not, but I can't help but think this is my

45

chance. How many times do you get a second chance to right a wrong?

We no longer have the problem of the university and me being her TA. Sure, we're going after the same job, but that's a problem for later.

Chapter Eight

I put my carry-on in the overhead bin and slide into my first-class window seat. Thank you, Mancini Advertising. They sure know how to treat their prospects.

Kenzie stands from her seat across the aisle. "Excuse me, I just have to get over there quickly." She slides in front of the man working his way down the row and throws herself into the seat next to me. "Tell me everything."

I look past her at Andrew, who is feeding Nolan cereal as he sits in Kenzie's now-empty seat.

I really don't want to get into this conversation. I'm still processing how all of this came about. And I know Kenzie, but it's not as though she's my best friend or anything. Hello, I didn't even know Andrew's cousin was coming on vacation with us, let alone that it was Pierce. And why didn't my family tell me we had an extra person joining us?

But I can see from the gleam in Kenzie's eyes that she's not going to let this go, so I figure I might as well get it over with.

"I studied abroad for a semester, and I met Pierce at a pub. It was a long time ago."

She smiles and good-naturedly rolls her eyes. "I know there's more to this story."

I shrug, not wanting to say it out loud because it sounds stupid. I lean forward, and Kenzie puts her hand on my arm.

"We hooked up one weekend, then I went to class and found out he was my teacher's assistant."

Her eyes widen, and she yelps. "Seriously?"

I nod, looking at the long line of passengers filing onto the plane. He hasn't gotten on yet, and I have a bad feeling that he's going to be seated in first class too. Mancini Advertising no doubt booked his ticket as well.

My gaze returns to Kenzie. Oh shit, no one has asked her to move because she's in their seat.

"Oh, I love it. Just when I thought this would be a relaxing holiday in the mountains—bam, you two are gonna spice it up."

"No, we're not." I place my hand over hers on my arm. "Pierce and I are very much over."

"Okay," she sing-songs.

"I'm serious, Kenzie."

"If you say so." She shrugs with a wide smile.

"I do."

"Maybe that's what you'll be saying to him some day." She giggles.

My eyes widen. "Stop."

"Pierce really is sweet. From what Andrew told me, he didn't have it easy when he was younger. Andrew's really happy to have Pierce here for the holiday season. Said otherwise he'd be by himself except for dinner on Christmas Day. It pulled at my heartstrings, you know? I love Christmas. Makes you extra grateful for what you have."

I pretend to not be fazed by what she's telling me, but my chest squeezes nonetheless. I had no clue. Pierce let me talk about my family a lot, but I realize that he never said anything about his own. He talked about his friends and funny stories, but not much else.

No. I cannot soften toward this man. I just have to get through the next week without being alone with him. As long as we're surrounded by people all the time, it will be fine. Completely fine.

"I think you're in my seat." We both look up to see Pierce standing at the end of the aisle.

"This is your seat?" Kenzie points at where she's sitting.

He flashes his phone with the seat assignment. "Appears so."

Great. Now I'm stuck side by side with him for five hours.

"You can sit with Andrew. Kenzie can sit here." I grip Kenzie's hand.

She turns across the aisle to look at Andrew, who shakes his head.

"Please keep the line moving so we can leave at our scheduled departure time," the flight attendant says over the speaker.

"Kenzie," Andrew says, tilting his head.

She looks back at me and cringes. "I'm sorry. If I stay here, I might not be married by the time we land. I'm just across the aisle." She springs up and moves to sit across the aisle.

It's fine. I mean, I can totally spend five hours next to Pierce. It's an evening flight, and I'm exhausted. I'll just sleep, or pretend to sleep, until we land.

Pierce slips into the seat with a grace not many can accomplish, or maybe it's just me who always feels as if I tumble into mine. He pulls out his AirPods, which I'm thankful for, and places them between his legs.

I try not to pay attention to him, crossing my legs and opening my book, but my thoughts get away from me, and the side of me that refuses to be quiet comes out. I inwardly curse her.

"Did you know this entire time? Did you somehow arrange this with Enzo Mancini? You two seemed pretty cozy after your interview."

He turns, rearing his head back, and I earn a quizzical look from the woman waiting in the aisle to continue her way past us. I'm not sure if the line has stalled or if she just wants to watch the show.

"Are you mad? Of course I had no idea. It's a coincidence, but then is it really? Of course Mancini would want you. And of course he'd want me too. We shouldn't be surprised he reached out to both of us."

I guffaw. "You don't know anything about my career. I work for a small firm in Portland." I bury my head back in my book.

"I know what kind of student you were."

"For one semester, and you used to dissect everything I did. You were so paranoid that people would find out about us that you acted as if I was stupid, picked on me when it was your day to lecture, and cut every piece of work I handed in to pieces."

"Is that what you think?" He turns to face me and leans in.

"Everyone knew you hated me. Said I challenged too much and that you wanted to put me in my place." I slam my book closed. I've only read the first line so far.

"I called on you because you were the smartest one in the class. I called on you because you were up for the challenge, and I enjoyed hearing your take on things."

"Whatever," I say, not wanting to hear what he's saying. Who knows if it's a lie or not? "We're stuck on this holiday together, so let's just keep our distance from each other."

"And if I don't want to?" He arches an eyebrow.

A sound of excitement comes across the aisle, and I look over to see Kenzie staring directly at us. Great, we have an audience. An audience who is probably going to tell my brother and Tessa everything we say here.

"It's too late, Pierce. I can't deny it, our time was..." I shake my head, not wanting to relive that memory. "But it's over. It's been six years, and this isn't some sign from the universe giving us another chance. Like the first time was the wrong time, and this is the right time. When we first met, I was Tre's sister, and you were Andrew's cousin. No cosmic force planned to have Andrew meet Kenzie and in turn Tre to meet Tessa in some weird plan to get us back together. So, just put your AirPods in and enjoy your flight."

I open my book.

Surprisingly, he doesn't say anything, but he reaches into his bag, pulls out a bag of Skittles, and places it in my lap.

My shoulders sink, and I murmur, "Thank you."

"You're welcome."

He puts his AirPods in his ears, presses his thumb to his screen, and scrolls.

We take off, and the airplane remains dark except for the light of screens and Andrew reading under the overhead light, Nolan asleep in his arms. Kenzie watches a movie on her phone propped up in the holder.

I turn my body toward the window, giving Pierce my back, but I feel his presence. I'd never tell him, but I so desperately want to feel his body against mine again. My mind drifts to that night for what feels like the millionth time since we ran into one another at the hotel.

His body pressed me against the door, caging me in. He took my hands, raised them up over us, and clenched his fingers through mine above my head, while his lips remained on mine.

I'd never been kissed the way Pierce kissed me. At that time,

I thought it was my innocence, but now, six years later, I know that isn't true.

Pierce was just an exceptional kisser. I'd never felt so wanted and desired as I did that weekend with him. Never felt so hopeful about what the future could bring.

His hands tightened in mine, and he ground his hardened length against me. The knowledge that he was that hard for me was an aphrodisiac I wasn't prepared to feel. It spurred my own hunger for him.

He stripped his lips off mine, not letting my hands go, and trailed his lips over my jaw. "God, I want to take my time with you, but I'm not sure I have the patience."

I knew how he felt. I didn't want it to end. I wanted to savor this, us, the first time I'd feel his fingers on me, in me, his lips over my body, his cock inside me. But I also wanted to sink to my knees, unbutton his pants, and get him so hot that he'd lose all control.

He nipped at my neck, and my eyes fell shut, allowing him to take me out of my thoughts and just feel *him. He was perfect in every way. Eventually, his hands unwound from mine, and his fingers glided down my arms, wrapping around my waist and tugging me against him.*

"Bedroom, okay?" he whispered.

All I could do was nod. His mouth didn't stop exploring my neck as he turned me around and walked me backward down a hall. I allowed him to lead me blindly, trusting this man I had just met. As though he couldn't stop himself, he stopped halfway, and again my back was to the wall, his hands on the hem of my shirt.

"Tell me if you're not ready," he said. He'd done that all night. Asked and questioned if I wanted this.

"I'm ready. I want this." I tried to make it clear, and he raised my shirt. Once it was off, he dropped it somewhere and drew back, his eyes soaking me in wearing only my bra.

"How in the bloody hell did I get you to agree to come home with me?" He took my hand and led me the rest of the way to his bedroom. He placed me on the edge of his bed, and we both toed out of our shoes. I reached back to undo my bra, thinking this was the moment we'd strip and have sex, but he surprised me by stepping forward, reaching around and placing his hand over mine. "May I?"

I slid my hands away from his and lowered my arms down to my sides.

"I've thought about nothing all night but what it would be like to strip you down." With one hand, he unclasped my bra, and it loosened around my chest. His hands rose to my shoulders and lowered the straps as his eyes followed their path, eventually leaving my chest bare before him. "As perfect as I imagined."

God, who was this guy? I was jealous of his word choices, the way he made me feel so beautiful while never actually saying the word.

I thought he'd reach for my breasts, but he broke the distance, his hand cupping my cheek and his lips finding mine again. He nudged me until I fell to his mattress, but he came along with me, his delicious weight pressing me into the softness.

From there it was a blur—clothes off, hands searching, touching, and caressing. His sweet words of how much he'd wanted all night to be right where we were. That the moment he saw me in the bar, he wanted to know how I tasted.

He pulled a condom from the nightstand and situated himself between my thighs. With his eyes on me and his hand on my hip, he pushed and slid inside me. Nothing had ever felt that good. I circled my hips, getting used to his size.

"God, Pierce," I said.

I'm jolted awake and out of my memory by something, and when I look around, I find Pierce smirking at me.

"What, pray tell, are you dreaming about?"

My face heats. There's no way he knows. "It was a nightmare actually. Apparently, I'm still in it."

He laughs. "I didn't realize you moan when you're scared. I quite enjoy hearing my name and God in the same sentence."

"It's not what you think," I snipe, although what I wouldn't do to escape back to the memory of him inside me.

"If you say so."

I look across to see the Wainwrights asleep, wishing I still was. God help me, get me off this plane.

Chapter Nine

PIERCE

When we land, I stare at the bag of Skittles shoved in the pocket of the seat in front of her. She never touched them. Heaviness invades my chest.

The only thing buoying my mood right now is that she was either remembering our time together or dreaming of me because those two words, "God, Pierce," were in her throaty turned-on voice. That moment repeats through my head like the lyrics of a favorite song.

I allow her to head down the aisle first, after Kenzie and Andrew walk out with a wide-awake Nolan. They wait for their stroller while Brynn and I continue into the terminal to wait.

"Are you excited to see your family?" I ask.

"Yes. Where is your family this Christmas?" she asks. "Aren't they going to miss you?"

"Andrew is my family," I answer. A quick, easy answer that hopefully won't spur any more questions.

She turns toward me, and I recognize the determination in her eyes from when she was in my class. She's going to hit me

55

with a hard question. I don't think Andrew would have told her about my past, but I feel unprepared.

"Finally, let's go." Kenzie walks by us as Andrew pushes the stroller.

Thank God.

We fall in step behind them and go down to retrieve our luggage, then the rental car. By the time we're on the road, Brynn is on one side of Nolan's car seat, and I'm on the other. Not exactly what I was hoping for.

"I can drive," I say to Andrew. "That way you two can sit back here with the little guy."

"Have you ever driven in the States?" Andrew asks.

"I think the concept is the same as in Britain," I say. "Stay on your side of the road."

Brynn's head is buried in her phone, and I'm sure she's not paying us any attention. Maybe she's as exhausted as I am. The early wake-up for my interview, the lack of sleep I got last night, and the nerves from being around Brynn is a lot to handle. Although she's already the highlight of my trip even if she doesn't want anything to do with me.

"I can't wait to see it in the morning," Kenzie says, staring out the window into the dark.

There's a lot more snow here, that's for sure. I don't know much about where we're staying. Andrew didn't go into a lot of detail when he ambushed me into this trip.

My mistake was telling him I was coming for an interview right before the holidays. Before I could make up an excuse, he told me I should stay for a visit and come on a skiing holiday with him and Kenzie. I had no idea he was going with another family until I had already asked Mancini Advertising to book my return flight to Utah.

Who would have guessed I'd be lucky enough to be on holiday with Brynn?

"Let's play some Christmas carols." Kenzie has definitely found a little pep since the flight.

Nolan's feet kick up and down, and she grabs Andrew's phone that's hooked up to the vehicle for the GPS.

"Kenz, I don't know where I'm going," he says, reaching for the phone.

She giggles and doesn't give it to him. We swerve, but Andrew corrects immediately. They continue to go back and forth, and I'm not gonna lie, I really think I would've been the safer bet to drive.

"People will ask, how did Brynn die? Went off a mountain cliff because Kenzie wanted to listen to 'Rudolph the Red-Nosed Reindeer.'"

Kenzie scoffs and glares at Brynn. "Give me some credit. 'Santa Claus is Coming to Town.'" Her gaze travels to Nolan. "Our favorite, right, buddy?"

He squeals in excitement.

Andrew gets the phone in hand, and we're back on track.

"You guys are no fun." Kenzie huffs.

"Believe me, there will be a ton of Christmas fun once we get there." Brynn circles her head as if her neck hurts, her eyes landing on me.

"I'd be happy to work that out for you when we get there," I say.

Andrew and Kenzie talk in lower tones.

"I'm good, thanks." Brynn goes back to looking out the window at the pitch darkness except for the other cars on the road.

Andrew eventually hands Kenzie the phone and instructs her how not to change the screen on the dash so he can still read the map whilst she acts as DJ.

Nolan laughs as his mom pretends her fist is a microphone and sings. Soon she's leaning into Andrew, and he's smiling at

57

her the way a husband should his wife—as though she's his everything.

It doesn't take long for Brynn to join in, and hell, I finally do too, all of us singing "Jingle Bells" as we roll through the entrance of our resort. All the evergreen trees are wrapped in an array of twinkling lights. One tree red, another green, and another white.

"Oh, look at the lights, Nolan." Kenzie points toward the window, and his attention turns that way.

"So pretty," Brynn says.

I admire the wide-eyed innocent look on her face as she stares out the front window.

"You like Christmas," I say because anyone could tell she does from the look on her face. "You hide it well."

She chuckles. "I love spending it with my family. I was just bummed it was going to be different this year. Get ready, because as soon as we pull into the parking lot, we're going to be bombarded."

"By the Russells!" Kenzie puts up her hands and waves them. "You're going to love them, Pierce. They even get my stodgy old husband to participate in their games."

"Games?" I ask, panic stiffening my muscles.

The only family I've ever spent time around is Andrew's. My aunt and uncle are nice and loving, but there aren't a lot of other family members. Most often, it would just be the four of us for holiday break.

"Oh yeah, I hope you brought your game because the Russells have a competitiveness that could challenge an Olympian's."

"She's not lying, Pierce," Andrew chimes in, glancing over his shoulder at me.

A little warning would've been nice. He knows my history. Knows how uncomfortable I am around families.

Andrew rounds the primary lodge area and heads down

another road and up a steep hill toward a bunch of smaller buildings.

"That must be our shared area in the middle. It's so cute." Kenzie turns to Brynn with excitement etched in every feature of her face. "Come on. You know it is."

Brynn shrugs. "It does look nice."

Andrew parks the SUV and shuts off the engine. A barrage of people file out of the house before we've even opened the car doors.

"How many people are there?" I ask anyone who will answer me.

No one does, and we each file out of the vehicle. Kenzie runs up to a woman with long dark hair and hugs her. Brynn walks up to who I assume is her mum, and she envelops Brynn in a hug. Everyone huddles around, and I stand as witness, unsure how I feel about spending the next week with this family I don't know.

Close families do everything together. Close families are going to ask questions. Close families will want to get to know the new guy because they'll want me to feel comfortable, but I'll be anything but.

Andrew slides by me, getting Nolan out of his car seat.

"A little warning would've been nice," I whisper.

"Sorry, mate," Andrew says. "But had I told you, you wouldn't have come."

He's not wrong. "Why did you want me to come so badly?"

He unstraps Nolan and carries him out of the car. "Reinforcements. I'm sick of being the only English fella." He laughs and walks toward the group. "Come on, show them that sparkling personality of yours."

I follow him, and by now, Brynn and Kenzie have made the rounds. A woman and man, who I assume are Brynn's parents, approach. I really want to make a good impression on them even if we're not anything.

"Andrew!" The woman swarms him in a hug and kisses Nolan on the cheek. "He's adorable."

"Merry Christmas, Gwen," Andrew says and puts out his hand for Brynn's dad. "Abe." He shakes his hand. "This is my cousin, Pierce."

Gwen's face lights up in a welcoming smile, and a sick feeling hits my stomach. She's going to dig everything out of me, I just know it.

"Merry Christmas, Pierce. I'm Gwen. We're so thrilled you could join us." She opens her arms, and I'm unprepared when she hugs me. My body stiffens, and I pat her back as if I can't move my arms while her palms run up and down my back. "Relax, we'll take it easy on you."

Somehow, her words do calm my nerves that have become frazzled as fast as a handful of sparklers, one exploding after the other.

Her dad comes by and holds out his hand just as he did to Andrew. "Welcome. I'm Abner, but you can call me Abe."

I take his hand. "Thank you."

The rest of the family heads my way, and I meet Kenzie's best friend, Tessa, and her husband, Tre, who is Brynn's brother, along with their little girl, Ryah. Then I meet Brynn's other brother, Carter, and his girlfriend, Faith. I can't help but notice everyone is coupled up, even the two toddlers who are now being held face to face by their parents.

"Come on in. We have some snacks for you guys in case you're hungry." Abner waves toward the building.

"I really just want my villa. Which one is it?" Brynn looks around.

There's one big building in the middle that I think must house the gathering area and kitchen, then there are little villas circling it with plowed pathways to the middle building.

"Yeah, let's eat first," Gwen says and puts her arm around Brynn's shoulders, guiding her toward the building.

"Oh, no." Brynn circles out of her mum's hold. "What's going on?"

"Can you wait until we can get some popcorn?" Carter says, chuckling.

Faith lightly smacks his stomach with the back of her hand.

"Oh my god, just tell me," Brynn says, obviously knowing her family well.

"It's really not a big deal." Gwen glances in my direction.

I look behind me because I've pissed Brynn off enough, and I don't have anything to do with this. Brynn follows her mum's line of vision, and her eyebrows scrunch.

"I need to get Ryah inside," Tre says and walks toward the big house.

"Oh yeah, let me make her a bottle." Tessa follows him, waving Kenzie to follow her.

Carter rocks back on his heels and crosses his arms with a mischievous smile plastered on his face.

"So, um…" Gwen says.

"There was a mix-up, and there's only one villa left. We looked in town to see if we could find an AirBnB and at the other resorts, but they're completely sold out." Abe cringes. "It's the holidays. We thought maybe you and Pierce could share."

"What?" Brynn's mouth drops open.

Oh. This is terribly awkward. Andrew is still here, and I toss him a pissed-off look since he's the reason I'm in this mess. Although sharing a villa with Brynn isn't the worst thing that could happen, I'm sure she'll think it is.

"I know." Gwen raises her hands. "The only other option we could think of was if Pierce was to stay with Andrew." She looks at me, and I look over at Andrew.

"You really want to sleep in a room with a child who wakes up through the night?" My cousin arches an eyebrow.

"Good point," I grumble.

"I'm sure you don't want to stay with Carter," Gwen says.

"Um, she's not invited to stay with Faith and me unless she wants to hear—"

"Go inside, Carter," Abe says, pointing at the big house.

Carter laughs and takes Faith's hand, leading her inside. I see now that all the others are staring out the window.

"The couch pulls into a bed," Gwen adds in a hopeful voice.

"I can stay with you then," Brynn says to her mum with a hopeful expression.

Gwen sighs. "Our couch doesn't pull out, and..." She looks at her husband.

"And Dad's snoring." Brynn groans. Her gaze shoots to mine. "Fine," she grumbles. "Which one is ours?"

Andrew raises his eyebrows at me. Although I haven't been able to tell him the entire story with Brynn, he looks at me as though this is a good thing for me.

And maybe it is. Sure, Brynn is pissed off about this, but how much easier will it be to win her over if we're sharing the same villa? Thanks, Santa.

Chapter Ten

BRYNN

You've got to be kidding me.

The entire flight, I told myself I was going to put my attitude aside and enjoy this trip. That Pierce and I could keep our distance, and I wouldn't have to spend the entire time trying to resist his charms because fool me once, shame on you. Fool me twice, shame on me as they say.

I step closer to my parents. "You're okay with me staying with a stranger?" I whisper, but it's so damn quiet out here that I'm sure Pierce and Andrew can hear me. "He could be a serial killer."

My dad scoffs, rolling his eyes as if it's not a possibility.

"Brynn." Mom sighs.

"There has to be somewhere else I can stay. What's in there?" I motion toward the big building. "I'll sleep on the couch. Better yet, he can sleep on the couch."

My dad puts his hand on my shoulder. "No one is sleeping on a couch for the entire week. Plus, you wouldn't be able to sleep in at all. That's where the kitchen and big gathering area is. Everyone will be convening there."

I look back at Pierce and see the small smirk on his face as if he's content with the idea that we *will* be sharing a villa.

I inhale a deep breath.

"He's a stranger," I say in a low voice.

Pierce steps forward into my little bubble with my parents. "Actually, we're not."

I whip my head in his direction. Oh, he is not going to tell my parents about our one-weekend fling six years ago. My brothers would never let me hear the end of it.

"What do you mean?" My dad tilts his head.

Thank you, Dad.

"I was Brynn's teacher's assistant back at university when she studied in London."

"Say what?" Carter stops right before he's about to walk into the house, turns back around, and heads back our way.

"Leave, Carter," Dad scolds, pointing at the house.

"Did you say teacher's assistant?" My mom faces Pierce, giving him all her attention.

I glare at him and step between my mom and Pierce. "That doesn't mean he isn't a stranger. It's been six years."

"I can vouch for my cousin," Andrew says from behind me. "He's a good guy and would never—"

"Dad, I'm your baby girl." I give him my puppy dog eyes. Surely they'll pull at his heartstrings, and he'll see that there's another way.

My mom shakes her head, places her hand on my shoulder, and nudges me out of the way. "So, you two know one another?"

Of course she's not going to let this go. My mom loves to be in the know.

"Yes." Pierce nods. "It's quite funny really. We interviewed for the same job in New York. We reconnected, and this whole thing with the holiday is completely coincidental."

Mom's gaze floats to me, her eyes questioning whether

he's telling the truth. I nod. It's all very weird and unusual, but here we are.

"Well, that's something for sure. Sounds like a little Christmas magic, huh, Abe?"

I roll my eyes. "There's nothing going on between us." I wave my finger between Pierce and me, though he's now standing a little too close.

"I just meant that I'm sure it's nice for Pierce to know not only Andrew but you as well. It's Christmas, and you should be around friends and family. Now he's got both." My mom holds her arms out as if we're one big happy family.

And I know she's probably listing all the questions in her head to slam me with when we're alone. I'm fooling myself if I think the fact that Pierce and I had a fling is going to stay quiet this entire trip.

"Sure do. I've never forgotten Brynn. She really kept me on my toes that semester."

Stop laying it on so thick, Pierce.

"That's so sweet. We think she's pretty great too." Mom stares at me with pride in her eyes. Little does she know he's referring to how good I was in bed. "Then it's settled, let me show you to your villa. Abe can get you guys settled, Andrew."

"Great," Andrew says, and he and my dad head back to the SUV.

Mom bypasses me, linking arms with Pierce and following my dad and Andrew to the SUV. I trail behind them. We take our suitcases from the vehicle, and Andrew unstraps Pierce's skis from the roof.

"Oh, you're a skier?" Mom asks, pursing her lips while she looks at me.

Pierce doesn't miss a beat, which doesn't surprise me. "You're a snowboarder?"

"I am."

"Then I look forward to some friendly competition."

I burst out laughing.

Mom pulls up the handles of the suitcases to wheel them to our villa. "Oh, Pierce, you just flipped the switch. Our Brynn is pretty biased on which is better."

My dad walks the opposite way to head to Andrew and Kenzie's villa. I assume they're next to Tessa and Tre, which means I'm next to Carter and Faith. This week keeps on giving.

"I'm pretty passionate as well." Pierce winks at me, and I scowl in return.

"Let's go, guys. Wait until you see how your villa is decorated." Mom follows the path before I can ask her what she means.

Pierce props his skis on his shoulder, and I try really hard not to find that appealing. I mean, it's just skis. He wheels one of his suitcases while my mom has another one, and I have mine. My parents brought the rest of my stuff, so I assume it's in the villa.

We're the last small building on the left-hand side. It's outlined in colorful holiday lights, and there are stickers on the windows with Christmas sayings.

"It's a code to unlock, so I'll text it to you both so you'll have it if you forget it," my mom says. "Pierce, I'll need your number."

"Sure," he says from behind me.

She enters the code, and the door unlocks, so she walks in first and flicks on the lights. "Isn't it just so cute?"

I follow my mom, and she's right, it is cute. And small. I'm not sure how Pierce and I are going to navigate our way around here without bumping into one another constantly. There's no door between the couch and bedroom area. But there's a fireplace and a small counter with a pod coffee maker and a whole tray of hot cocoa fixings. Freshly baked Christmas cookies are on a tray with "Welcome" iced on the middle one.

"Very nice." If I wasn't staying with Pierce, I might say I love it and what a great decision it was to come here this year. But I fixate on the couch and how close it is to the bed.

"Marvelous." Pierce rests his skis along the wall in the corner behind the door. "This place is something, that's for sure. Good job, Gwen." He smiles at my mom, and she beams at his compliment.

I can't help but enjoy that he's buttering her up. She does a lot for us and deserves the praise for always taking care of our needs.

"Well, I'm glad you like it. I'm going to head over to the main lodge." She walks toward the door. "I'll send the code to Brynn, and we can exchange numbers up at the main lodge."

Pierce shakes his head. "Brynn has my number, so she can forward it to me. No problem there."

"She does?" Mom does a terrible job of hiding her smile.

I see her mind spinning with possibilities. "He just got it at the airport. I haven't been hiding him in London for the past six years. We'll be up soon. Thanks, Mom."

She smiles and looks at me for a moment as if she's relieved. Knowing her, she probably is. All three of her children are now here. "Don't take too long. The babies are all out of whack, so we were thinking about playing a game and calling it a night."

"I have to take a raincheck. With the time difference..." Pierce says.

Thank goodness he's not going to tag along to every event we have.

"Oh, I understand. Abe and I went to Europe once, and it took forever to get over my jet lag. But I do hope you'll join us tomorrow after you get some rest."

She leaves and shuts the door. I remain near the bed while he stays by the sofa.

"Want to flip for it?" I open my purse to grab a coin.

"Give me some credit. You take the bed, and I'll take the sofa bed."

"If you're sure. We could swap halfway through the week." It's my halfhearted attempt to meet him halfway.

He sits on the arm of the couch and stares at me, clasping his hands in his lap. "I understand that this isn't ideal, but I don't want us tiptoeing around one another for the next week."

"There isn't anything wrong," I say, lying through my teeth.

"Okay, I don't want to constantly feel as though I'm spoiling your holiday."

I nod. He has a point.

"Truth?" I sigh.

He nods. "Please."

"It hurt. It sucked when I walked into that classroom, and my stomach filled with an exhibit of butterflies seeing you in that first row. And when you didn't smile, but I witnessed your smile actually fall, it cut me. I think I knew then, but once it was confirmed by Professor Jorgensen about you being the TA, I thought we'd have a conversation about what it meant. It was only one semester." It feels good to finally get my feelings out there.

He pushes a hand through his dark hair. "I wish I had handled it differently, but Professor Jorgensen had a lot of control over where students ended up. I was afraid that if he found out, he wouldn't believe that things happened before I knew you were a student. So I distanced myself completely. I'm sorry."

His green eyes that drew me in that first night shine like the North Star, and my defenses crumble. "Okay then."

"But Brynn." He stands. His height is one thing I loved about him. The way his body sheltered mine when he pressed me to the door. "I have nothing to fear now. I made the mistake of letting you slip out of my grasp once. I'm not making the same mistake twice."

My pulse skyrockets. "We can't."

"Why not?"

I pick up my suitcase, put it on the luggage holder, and turn my back to him because if I have to look at him, I might not say it. "There is not a second chance for us."

"Give me a reason." I hear his footsteps walk closer to me.

"I don't even know you."

"We can change that." His breath floats over my bare neck.

"I'm not looking for just sex. My vibrator gets the job done just fine."

He chuckles, and I close my eyes to gain my bearings.

"Turn around, Brynn," he says softly.

"What?" I circle around and straighten my back, crossing my arms.

"We both know you aren't satisfied with your vibrator. The sex between us was something I've never experienced before or since. I bet it's been the same for you. So, I'll give you a little bit of space, but I have an entire week to prove to you that we belong together. Get ready."

My chest tightens, and I let out a sarcastic laugh to play off how much his words affect me. "Ready for what?"

"For you to fall in love with me."

"You're crazy." I laugh again and spin around, but he grabs my wrist, his thumb running over the skin on the inside. We stand in place, and he steps closer, his front to my back.

"There hasn't been a day you haven't crossed my mind."

"Well, sorry, I'm not on the market."

He frowns. "You're not single?"

I smirk at him. "Maybe I should have been more specific. I'm not on the market *for you*."

I shut my suitcase with my free hand, wind my wrist out of his grasp, and beeline it to the door.

Once I'm on the other side, I lean my back against the door, close my eyes, and inhale a few deep breaths of the cold air.

Seven days.

I can do anything for seven days. Even resist the only man who's ever really had the power to hurt me.

Chapter Eleven

PIERCE

The sofa bed turns out to have the worst mattress I've ever slept on, so I toss and turn all night, listening to Brynn's soft breathing in the dark. She's so close that the desire to crawl in beside her and wrap my arms around her is a constant itch under my skin.

Today has been a complete whirlwind. I stare at the ceiling, trying to process that she's here in the flesh. The one woman who has floated in and out of my mind every day since she left London.

I'm a smart man, and I don't necessarily believe in soulmates. To many, it would sound stupid that one woman, one weekend could hold so much reverence, but that weekend was filled with magic. I can't explain it.

But as I try to find sleep, my mind refuses to listen, and it floats to the morning after I brought her home and my desperation to make sure she didn't leave.

A hand flung over my chest and a pile of hair in my mouth. My eyes sprang open to feel Brynn's soft body wrapped around me.

Her leg slid up my thigh, her knee gliding along my length that was already up and ready, but she spurred him into wanting action now.

I ran my hand down her back, thankful she hadn't snuck out on me. I kissed the top of her head as if she'd been mine for years. She purred and tightened her arm around my middle.

"Spend the day with me?" I asked, putting myself and my intentions out there.

It was an unusual act for me, and I believed that the therapy I'd been going to for the past few years was finally working because I wanted to see where this went with Brynn. Following a connection was something I struggled with, but developing one so quickly was even more out of character for me.

She picked her head up, resting her chin on my chest, and stared at me for a long time. I bent one arm along my pillow, my hand cradling my head to meet her eyes.

"Okay," she said, and I couldn't believe she accepted.

I flipped her to her back, and she yelped, giggling until I widened her legs with my thighs, spreading her open. I slid my body down the length of hers, pushing her thighs further to fit my shoulders, and I lost myself in her for another hour before I had enough willpower to get out of bed.

We showered, and I made her some toast before we headed out of the house.

"This feels weird," she said, fixing the T-shirt I'd given her to wear.

"I wish you would have worn my boxers." I swung my arm around her waist and tugged her closer to me.

"Why?" Her head rested on my shoulder, and she stared up at me, her brown eyes making my breath hitch.

"Because now I have to try not to think about how you don't have any knickers on all day. Imagine if you had worn a dress last night." I groaned.

She smiled up at me, and a thrill shot through my body. It hadn't even been twenty-four hours, and I already knew it was different. She was different.

"We could go back to your place." Her finger trailed down the front of my shirt.

"We will, but let's get you that coffee first."

"Yes, please."

I directed her into the small café on the corner by my flat. It was busy since it was Sunday, and we stood in line with her arms around my waist, my arm slung around her, pressing her to my body as though we were in love. And it felt really bloody good that she seemed to be as into me as I was into her. On a normal day, I would have been annoyed to spend so long in line, but with her, I could have stayed there forever.

We stepped up when it was our turn, and she rambled off her coffee order, as I did mine. I paid, then we followed the line and waited for my name to be called, still in each other's arms. My name was called, and I reluctantly broke apart from her and grabbed our coffees, taking them both to the counter with the milk and sugar.

She added a bit of cream, but no sugar.

I added cream and some cinnamon to mine.

"You're adding cinnamon?" she asked.

I nodded, holding it out for her.

"Can I try yours first to see if I like it?" She held out her hand, and I passed my coffee to her.

I watched her lips cover the rim of the cup, remembering them wrapped around my cock the night before.

Her eyes widened. "That's so good." She went to hand me back my coffee, but I shooed the cup away.

"Take it." I picked up hers and added cinnamon to it.

We walked out of the café, and she couldn't stop remarking about how delicious the coffee was with cinnamon. I had to admit, I liked that I was able to introduce her to something new.

I led her to a park, and we sat on a bench, people watching while we drank our coffee.

"Tell me something about you," she asked.

We'd shared silly superficial things about one another the night before. I wanted to get to know her better, but at the same time, I loved that she didn't know everything about my past. It tended to make people feel sorry for me, and I hated it.

"What do you want to know?"

"I don't know." She shrugged. "Tell me a food you hate that most people love."

I chuckled and shook my head. "Pizza. I'm not a pizza guy."

She balked. "How is that possible? Maybe you just haven't had the right pizza."

"That's what everyone says. If it has dough, cheese, and sauce, I'm not a fan."

She dropped her feet to the cement to stand, pretending she was going to walk away. "Sorry, I gotta go."

I tugged on the back of her light jacket, and she fell to my side, laughing.

"Fine, I'll try pizza," I said because I'd do about anything to keep her right next to me.

"Look how we're compromising." She laughed again, and I tried to commit the sound to memory.

"So, what can't I force you to eat?" I swung my arm over her shoulder to make sure she didn't leave.

"Chocolate cake." She cringed.

"I'm not really a cake person, so you're safe there."

She flipped around and propped one leg up on the bench, staring at me as if it might actually be the last straw. "How do you not like cake?"

"You just said you didn't." I chuckled.

"Chocolate cake I don't like. But give me a white cake, a yellow cake. One filled with strawberries and whipped cream."

Her eyes rolled back in her head like they had when she came this morning.

"You're making me jealous of cake."

Her hand splayed on my chest, her fingers trailing down the front of my shirt. She did that often, and I was really starting to love the casualness and closeness I felt.

"Oh, well, I like other things more than cake." Her fingers continued their trail, dipping under the waistband of my jeans.

I looked around, but no one was paying us any attention. "Keep it up, and I'm going to throw you over my shoulder and lock you in my flat."

Her head reared back in laughter. God, she was beautiful. I couldn't believe she'd agreed to spend the day with me.

We finished our coffees, continuing to rank foods from our favorite to our least, never agreeing on one.

After throwing away our cups, we walked through the city, me pointing out little things to her. Every time her eyes lit up with interest, my chest puffed out, loving that I was the one introducing her to my city.

She pulled me into a small shop that looked more for tourists than locals, and I trailed behind her as she browsed. I couldn't stop looking at her, committing her facial expressions to memory. Her excitement, her smiles, the way she would glance over her shoulder to make sure I was still there. I'd been closed off to almost everyone throughout my life, never allowing anyone to really know me, until her. It was as if she had a spell over me. I felt slightly out of control, and I didn't care.

I twirled a display and picked up a keychain that said I Heart London with the Union Jack on it.

"What's that?" Brynn came over and rested her head on my shoulder.

"A keychain I'm going to buy for you."

She picked it out of my hand and ran her fingers over the

words I Heart London. "You don't have to buy it for me. I can buy it."

"So, you like it?" I was unsure if she'd want it, but I felt she could take it home with her and remember our weekend.

I had no idea how long she was staying in London. If she was doing some kind of tour through Britain and Europe like so many Americans do. I should ask, but doing so would ultimately bring up the future and the fact that we didn't live in the same country. I was afraid to get too deep and ruin our time together before it was necessary.

"I love it." She went up to the checkout, and I slid my credit card across the counter.

"Pierce..."

I kissed her temple. "I want you to remember me," I said, sounding like a complete fool.

"Is this a goodbye gift?"

I stared into her eyes. "No."

The woman offered me a bag, but I shook my head and put the keychain in my pocket.

I felt as if we made a promise to one another right there. To allow ourselves that day in the bubble we'd created for each other. We'd deal with the questions of what it all meant later.

The problem was, we left that store, went back to my place, and spent the rest of our time in bed. We exchanged numbers when she said she had to leave my place on Sunday. And when she walked out my flat's door, I felt sure that we'd start dating and figure out how we fit in each other's lives.

But Monday changed everything.

I roll over and grip the pillow under my head, pushing the thoughts away so I don't have to think of what a wanker I was to her. How I was the one who ruined it.

Chapter Twelve

BRYNN

I wake up to an empty villa.

Pierce isn't on the sofa. In fact, the sofa bed is already tucked away, his blanket and pillow stacked neatly at one end of the couch.

Where would he have gone?

I flip my legs over the edge of the bed and stare out the window. The landscape is gorgeous. The mountains, the fresh snow, the green trees. I hate to admit it, but I think my family was on to something when they decided to come here for the holidays.

There are footsteps in the snow from our villa to the main lodge, and I notice then his coat isn't hung up on the coat tree next to the door. Guess he didn't feel like taking the shoveled path.

Pierce's suitcase sits open on the other luggage rack, and I have the urge to be nosey and take a peek, wanting to see some evidence of the man he is now.

I shake my head and go into the bathroom. His stuff sits neatly on one side of the counter—a contact case, toothbrush, razor, cologne. It feels oddly intimate to be sharing this space with him, even without him here.

Not wanting to leave him alone with my family since I know my mom will wake up early as she always does, I hurry to brush my teeth, finger-comb my hair into a messy bun, and throw on a sweatshirt over my flannel pajamas. After slipping my feet into my boots, I trudge out of our villa and make my way to the main lodge. The air is crisp and smells like pine trees.

I open the door to find my mom and dad on the big leather chairs by the window, admiring the light sprinkling of snow coming down.

"Good morning," I say, walking over to them and sitting in the other chair.

"Better in the daytime, right?" My dad points at the window.

"It really is something." I grab the blanket lying over the arm of the chair and pull it over my lap.

"So, do you want to tell us what's going on?" Mom asks, poking as she always does.

"What do you mean?" I don't look at her or my dad.

"You know, Brynn. How well exactly do you know your TA?"

I take a chance and glance at her. Sure enough, her eyebrows are raised. She's the worst, always knowing when something is going on.

But I don't get a chance to answer because the door opens, and Tessa walks in with my niece, Ryah. Since I spent no time with them last night, I throw the blanket off me and beeline it over to her.

"Hey, sweet girl," I say, holding out my arms.

Ryah comes to me easily, and I twirl her around, walking over to the circle of toys in the corner.

"I'm going to make her breakfast," Tessa says.

"I was just about to start. Heard the guys went to work out, so I was giving them some time." Mom swings her feet down from the chair and goes to stand.

"I'll just make her some eggs and get her some milk. Don't worry about it, Gwen." Tessa busies herself in the kitchen.

My mom relaxes back in her seat. This is her vacation as well, and I should remember that, since at home, she's always busy doing something. Dad pulls out his phone and starts playing some Christmas music on the stereo. He's so techy.

"My favorite," I say, keeping Ryah in my arms and dancing around the room.

She lays her head on my shoulder because she's likely still tired after last night and the disruption to her usual schedule.

"So..." Tessa says, and I know what she's going to say before she even says it. "Pierce?"

Mom laughs. "You're just in time! We were just starting the inquisition."

Tessa giggles and pulls out a pan. "He's really attractive. I mean, he's no Tre, but..."

"Ew, stop talking about my brother like that." I shrug. "Pierce is okay."

Tessa eyes me hard, not about to call me out, but she's telling me she knows he's more than okay in my book.

"He was her TA in London. Did you know that, Tessa?" Mom says, getting up from her chair and going into the kitchen because she can't help herself. She stops and kisses Ryah on the head.

Ryah tries to go to her, but I spin her around.

"Ohhh, scandalous. Tell me more." Tessa pours herself a cup of coffee, sips it, and pulls an egg out of the fridge.

"Nothing to tell. That's just how we know each other."

"Well, he's not looking at you like you're his student, that's for sure," Mom says.

"Let's remember that's my daughter you're talking about," Dad calls.

My mom turns to look back at him. "Oh hush, you have no problem talking about the boys."

"She's my little girl. I'm the only man in her life as far as I'm concerned."

I dance over to my dad and kiss his cheek. "You're always my number one."

He smiles at me, and this time, Ryah refuses to be persuaded away from my dad. He places his coffee cup on the table and holds out his arms for her. "Want to see the snow?"

Ryah gets comfortable on my dad's lap, and I go to sit on one of the bar stools at the kitchen island.

"Come on," Tessa whispers.

I know I can trust her. Seeing how her and Tre figured out their issues, she'd understand.

The door opens and a gush of cold wind comes in.

"Seriously, it's so cold out there." Kenzie holds Nolan, who's bundled up in his snowsuit. "He's going to get frostbite."

"You live in New York," Tessa deadpans.

"It's the wind here."

Tessa laughs. "Get him out of that suit, he's probably sweating." Tessa sips her coffee.

Mom takes over cracking the egg and scrambling it in a pan.

"I could be here childless enjoying a morning coffee, but someone's ex-military husband had to drag my husband out of bed when it was still dark. Who picks the holidays to start a workout regimen? Only Andrew." Kenzie shakes her head while we all laugh. "He took yours too." Kenzie places Nolan in the blocked off area with the toys.

He whines for Ryah, and my dad goes over there with the two of them to play. God, I love my parents.

"He's not mine," I say.

"I'm making Ryah an egg. Want me to make one for Nolan too?" my mom asks.

"Oh Gwen, I can—"

"Nonsense, I'm already here." My mom waves her off, then goes to the fridge to get another egg.

"Thank you, Gwen. You're spoiling me. Especially since Tessa should be making the eggs since she's the one who's allowing her husband to work out on vacation."

Tessa balks, and they laugh. "Trust me, you'll thank me later when his stamina is so good."

I cover my ears. "Okay, gross."

I'm really kidding. I got over the fact my brothers have a sex life a long time ago. I didn't really have a choice with Carter being the way he is.

"Talking about brothers and sex... who is Faith?" Kenzie asks.

"Flavor of the month?" I direct the question to my mom.

She huffs. "He says he likes this one." Her look says maybe not. "It hasn't been that long though."

I shouldn't judge. I'm still hung up on a guy I met six years ago and spent one weekend with.

"Speak of the devil," Tessa says, eyeing the door where Carter appears, the only guy besides my dad who didn't work out this morning.

He holds open the door for Faith. She's cute, but she's his typical type. A brunette who looks at him as though he can do no wrong. I'd like a woman who challenges him a bit.

"Someone skipped the workout," Kenzie says. "Good for you, Faith. Way to keep him in your bed. Want to do a quick tutorial later?"

Everyone laughs.

"It's the other way around. I keep her in bed. She wanted to go workout with the guys," Carter says, going over to the kid's area and kneeling next to my dad to play with the kids.

The thought of Faith in tight workout leggings, bending over in front of Pierce, ignites the embers of jealousy I didn't think still lived under my skin.

Mom finishes the eggs, and Tessa and Kenzie get their kids situated in their highchairs to eat. The door opens again, and the workout crew files in. My brother heads right over to Ryah, kissing her head and pretending to take her eggs. Then he goes over to Tessa and murmurs something in her ear. She pushes him away gently, talking about how sweaty he is.

Andrew does the exact same thing with Kenzie, except he tells her to get up off the chair and go relax, sitting in the seat next to Nolan to take over.

"You're all losers for working out," Carter says. "This is a vacation, and you all have women in your beds." He sits at the table.

"I didn't." Pierce eyes me as he grabs a water bottle from the fridge. His forearms flex as he opens it, and I admire the sweat coating his skin.

He looks good fresh off a workout. Why am I surprised? He always looked edible when he was sweaty from sex too.

"You should've brought someone," Carter says to Pierce. "Ouch."

I turn to see Carter rubbing his forearm.

"Jesus, Tessa, those nails of yours." Carter glares at her.

And there it is, my family thinking something is going to happen between Pierce and me. They've already put us together in their minds. Well, they're wrong.

"Did you have your coffee yet?" Pierce asks me in a low voice, crushing his empty water bottle and tossing it in the recycling.

The conversation continues as they all talk about plans and when to hit the slopes.

Mom pulls out the ingredients for pancakes, eggs, and bacon. She's obviously going to make a big breakfast.

Pierce goes to the coffee pot at the beverage station, takes two mugs, and pours coffee, then goes about doctoring them. "Gwen, I'd be happy to make breakfast," he says, sliding a cup my way.

Mom watches him, trying to hide her smile.

I stare at the cup, and my breath hitches. Pierce doesn't say anything. He doesn't remark about the fact that he made it just how I take it. That six years have passed, and he still remembers I like a little bit of cream... and cinnamon, ever since he introduced me to it.

Mom bends forward over the island, staring into my cup. She falls back onto her heels and raises her eyebrows. "Is that the English way of drinking coffee?"

"The cinnamon?" he asks before sipping his cup.

"I was surprised when Brynn returned from London insisting she couldn't drink coffee without cinnamon in it." She leans her hip on the counter. "I mean, people here drink it too, but is it more common there?"

"I don't think so."

"But you drink it with cinnamon too?" my mom asks.

"Cinnamon? I've never tried it like that." Kenzie comes over and looks into my cup. "You both take your coffee the same way?"

Kenzie glances at Tessa, and they exchange a look.

"It's fairly common. They have cinnamon available in all the cafés for a reason." I roll my eyes, sipping my coffee that somehow tastes better since he made it.

"I don't know anyone else who does that, do you, Tessa?" Kenzie asks.

I grind my teeth together.

"Nope." Tessa shakes her head, both of them looking at me.

"I do. My boss drinks it that way," Faith says. "And she's really picky about the brand."

Tessa and Kenzie glance in her direction as though she doesn't get what they're saying.

"It's very sweet and kind of like kismet that you both drink it the same way, but my question is how does Pierce know you like cinnamon in your coffee?" Mom asks.

My gut twists.

The room quiets. Even Nolan and Ryah stop babbling to one another.

I glare at Pierce because he better fix this. I am not interested in spending my entire holiday with my family in setup mode.

"I can do the pancakes," Pierce says, dodging the question.

Thankfully, Ryah takes it upon herself to scream at that exact moment, and everyone turns back to them to see what the problem is. But I know my family. These questions aren't going to go away until they get the answers they want.

Chapter Thirteen

PIERCE

She thinks I don't see the way she looks at me, but I keep catching glimpses when she thinks I'm not looking.

I took a chance on her coffee, hoping like hell she didn't strip cinnamon from her coffee because of me. Gwen confirmed it though—Brynn has drunk cinnamon in her coffee ever since she got back from London.

Everyone has eaten, and I really want to go shower, but Gwen and Abe stop Carter and Faith when they're about to leave, saying we have business to attend to. I'm not sure what that means, but all three of their biological kids groan, then sigh dramatically. Kenzie, however, straightens in her chair and claps.

Andrew comes alongside me, holding his coffee mug. "Get ready for this."

"What?"

"The competition thing I told you about. We'll hit the slopes after. Kenzie said she's staying back today with Nolan. She's into some book that she wants to finish while he naps."

"Awesome, can't wait to ski after coming back from a full body workout."

We rest our backs along the wall, each holding our coffee mugs, waiting for the announcement or whatever is about to happen.

Abe sets up his laptop while Gwen turns on the television, and they share a look that causes the hairs on the back of my neck to stand up.

I've kept myself distracted in the kitchen, which is why I offered to help Gwen prepare breakfast for everyone. Then I cleaned the dishes with the help of Carter and Faith. Every day while we're here, two people will be assigned to clean, and it's never Gwen, which is fair since she says she'll do most of the cooking. But keeping myself busy keeps me from interacting with all of them. They're wonderful people, I just don't know them well.

Brynn sits on the edge of the couch.

"Come on." Gwen waves everyone over.

Ryah and Nolan are in their play area, and the rest of the people move over in front of the fireplace with the television over it. There are stockings hung along the mantel that appear to be homemade and each have a family member's name. Andrew, Kenzie, and Nolan each have one too, although theirs appear to be newer than all the Russells.

"Hey, you two, you're part of this too." Gwen signals for us to join.

I stand behind Brynn, but not too close, while Andrew stands right next to Kenzie, wrapping his arm around her waist.

"Since our family is growing by the year, and we have some extra guests this year, our annual Christmas competition is going be in teams." She presses a button on the computer, and a slide show starts on the TV screen.

She and Abe took the time to do a slideshow? Is this a normal thing families do?

Listed on the screen are the teams paired in twos.

"Mom..." Brynn says because she sees what I do.

"I'm sorry, but at the time, we weren't aware of you both knowing one another with some secret past where he knows your coffee order. It made sense."

Each team is made of one of the couples, except for Brynn and me. We're a team.

"We should be drawing numbers," Brynn says.

"Don't be sour. Faith wouldn't wanna be with any of you competitive jerks." Carter kisses her cheek.

"Seriously? You're the biggest competitor," Brynn snipes.

"I'm not. Tre is," Carter argues.

"Can we please not?" Gwen interrupts. "So, these are the events. We're going to have a gingerbread house decorating contest, fastest couple to make a snowman, sugar cookie decorating contest, scavenger hunt, ski and snowboard switch, and since Carter won last year, he gets to pick the final contest. I emailed him last month, and..." Gwen puts out her hand as if Carter's got the floor.

With his happy-go-lucky personality, I can only imagine what he'd pick.

He scoots Faith from his lap and slips out of the chair, running his hands together like an evil genius.

"Oh jeez, just spit it out," Tre says, shaking his head.

"Yeah, get on with it. Just tell us what ridiculous thing you picked." Brynn sips her coffee, and a small sigh slips out of her. It pierces something inside me I'm not ready to investigate yet.

"It has to be Christmas-related, remember." Abe chimes in.

"Oh, it is." Carter waggles his eyebrows.

"Let's go, we'd like to get on with our day," Tessa says.

"The competition will be to see who can melt an ice sculpture the fastest." He laughs and turns to Faith, who joins in on his laughter as if they thought about it together.

"That's easy. Hairdryer." Kenzie rolls her eyes.

"Nope. Hands and mouth are the only things you can use. And thank Faith, because I wanted it to be mouths only."

"Only you, Carter." Brynn gets off the end of the couch, running right into me like she did at the airport.

My hands hold her upper arms to steady her, and she looks up at me.

"Sorry," she says, garnering the attention of her family.

I release my hold, and she goes back to the drink station, making herself another coffee.

When I look away from her and back at the room, I find each family member staring at me. Andrew especially. I can already tell he's going to ask me more questions about my time with Brynn.

"Mind your own business," Brynn calls out behind me. "So, when does this start?"

Gwen gives me a soft smile and signals to Abe for the next slide. "Yes, I know you're all itching to get out there. Tonight, we'll do the tree decorating. After all, it's not Christmas without a tree. Everything will be delivered to your villas. It's a craft, so a lot of construction paper, glue, and other items. If you have anything bought from a store..." Everyone looks at Carter, and he groans. "You're disqualified. Got it?"

"What do you get if you win?" I ask. I'm not hoping for some monetary value or prize, just curious. Since they all take it so seriously, it must be something big.

The entire room laughs except for the kids.

"Tell him what you won last year, Carter," Tre says as if he's razzing him, but it's clear he's just as competitive as his brother.

"You get your picture on the star on top of the tree the next year."

"Which does bring up..." Gwen walks over to a box and digs out a gold star. "Go ahead and put it on the tree."

"My pleasure." Carter takes it from his mother, then grabs the ottoman next to the couch and stands on it to place it on top of the tree.

This family is bonkers. All of this for your picture on a star? Absurd.

Brynn walks by with her coffee and examines the gold star with Carter's smiling face in the middle. "Did you get that professionally done?"

"I haven't won in, like, five years. It was a big moment." Carter grins.

"I think you need to find more purpose in your life." Brynn walks past me, ignores me, and sits back on the edge of the sofa.

"Maybe my purpose should be to find out what really happened in London." Carter puts up a finger. "Was Pierce more than your TA? Pretty sure he was, but we're waiting for you to give us all the deets."

"Shut up," she says.

"Okay, you two," Gwen says to them. "Every day, the competition will be presented to keep you on your toes. Go about your merry days now."

Abe turns off the computer and Gwen the television.

Andrew comes over to me. "Let's go. Who else is heading out?"

Carter, Faith, Abe, Gwen, and Tre all raise their hands.

"We'll meet in, like, forty-five?" Tre offers.

"Perfect." Andrew nods.

Brynn slides into the corner of the couch.

"You're not going?" I ask her.

She shakes her head. "Not yet. Tre said he'll be back at lunch, then I'll go out with Tessa for a bit. Have fun on your skis."

I bend down so only she hears me. Everyone else is busy talking to their significant other. "One of these days, we're going to have a race, and if I win, I want a lot more than my picture on a star."

Her breath hitches, but she schools her features. "Sure, and don't worry, I'll go easy on you."

I chuckle in her ear. "That's a shame because I plan on giving it to you hard."

I straighten and walk out of the main lodge, wishing she was coming with me. As it is, I'm going to have to rub one out in the shower to ease the tension in my body.

The woman drives me crazy. In the best way.

Chapter Fourteen

BRYNN

Let the inquisition begin. I purposely didn't leave with the rest of my family because I need some advice from Tessa and Kenzie without my mom's involvement. There will be a time to tell her everything, but I need to process all of this first.

Ryah and Nolan grow sleepy, their moms picking them up and cuddling them. I'm not sure I'm ready for a family, but it sure looks nice on them.

"Spill it, girl," Tessa says.

I pick up a pillow from the couch and put it over my face, my cheeks heating.

"You two are totally hot together."

I drop the pillow as Kenzie looks at Tessa, who nods.

"He remembered your coffee order," Tessa coos.

I roll my eyes, picking up my coffee mug and sipping the flavor he introduced me to. "Well, I could have easily never drunk it again after what happened."

"What did happen?" Kenzie asks.

I blow out a breath. "I went to London to study abroad for a semester. My first weekend there, I met Pierce at a pub, spent the weekend with him, and... we connected." I look between my sister-in-law and her best friend.

"No judgment here. It only took your brother a cross-country road trip to make me fall for him." Tessa kisses Ryah's head.

"I can't even describe it. It sounds unrealistic and completely naive. I was young and stupid and thought that... I don't know." I sip my coffee.

They give me a sympathetic look.

"Just because you were young doesn't mean it wasn't real." Kenzie lays Nolan on the couch between us, putting a pillow on the side just in case. "The heart feels what it feels. Age has no bearing."

"You writing greeting cards now?" Tessa laughs.

"Sometimes it's just the wrong timing." Kenzie raises her eyebrows at me.

"It was definitely the wrong timing, but I'm worried it was more because I was in a foreign country, and I was clinging to a connection I found because I was homesick. After finding out he was my TA, I felt completely alone again."

"We can all figure out how you both fell for one another, but tell us the problem. Why aren't you acting on your attraction to him now?" Tessa stands and takes Ryah to the pack-n-play in the corner, then pours herself another cup of coffee before sitting with her legs crossed in the chair.

"The problem? Which one?"

"The reason why you're hiding your excitement about this coincidental reconnection." Tessa arches an eyebrow over her mug.

I narrow my eyes at her. "I'm not excited."

"Yeah, and I wasn't excited when Andrew showed up at my brother's for Thanksgiving either." Kenzie bursts out laughing. Nolan stirs, but when Kenzie puts her hand on his tummy, he calms back down.

"Yeah, I wasn't excited when Tre bailed me out of jail either," Tessa says.

They both laugh, and I toss a wadded napkin at Kenzie since she's closer. It falls on Nolan.

"Trying to kill my kid?" she jokes.

They both sober up and stare at me. I guess it's time I let myself remember the humiliation I felt that day. If anything, it will help solidify exactly why I shouldn't give him another chance.

I'd woken to a text message from Pierce asking how it was possible that having me in his bed for two nights had already ruined him. He wanted to see me that night and said he'd be available for dinner.

I stopped at the café, ordered a coffee, and added cinnamon, thinking of him and the comfort I'd felt around him that weekend. I'd never been someone who got close to someone I was dating really fast. I made friends quickly, but when it came to relationships, they were slow to build. Mostly because I was the youngest Russell. The little sister of Tre and Carter. The boys I'd grown up with had been intimidated by that fact.

And truth was, if they didn't want to date me because they were scared of my brothers, then I didn't want to date them anyway.

I was pretty sure I was in this love bubble that Pierce had built around us.

We figured out when and where we'd go to dinner, and I told him I'd meet him there, but he said he wanted to pick me up. I sent him my address and that's where our messages left off.

I walked into my first class of the day excited to finally take some classes that had to do with my major, unlike my freshman year back at the University of Oregon. The minute I stepped into the room and stood at the top of the stairs of the lecture hall, something felt different, but I couldn't put my finger on it.

I stepped down to the first row because I was the kind of student who wanted to be front and center, and that's when I stopped dead in my tracks.

Pierce was standing at the end of the other row, his gaze on me as if it had followed me since I walked through the door.

I smiled, wondering why he was in this class, but we'd never talked about what each of us did. I thought maybe he'd started school late since he was older than me, but what were the chances we'd be in the same class? At the same time, I didn't care. I was just elated to see him.

"Hey," I said, and he looked over his shoulder as though he was checking for someone.

I noticed right away that the energy around him was different than the weekend, different even than his morning texts.

"I thought you were a tourist?" he asked in a blunt tone that made me draw back.

"Yeah, kind of. I'm studying abroad this semester." I smiled like an idiot who wasn't connecting the dots.

"So, you're in this class?"

I nodded then forced a smile. "Are you too? Want to sit next to each other? I promise not to cheat." I laughed, but he didn't, and my stomach sunk.

Oh my god, he had a girlfriend. Although there had been no trace of another woman at his flat, I figured that had to be it.

"Is she in this class?" I asked, attempting to restrain my fury.

His head reared back, and he stared at me the way I assumed I was staring at him. Both of us confused. "What?"

I didn't appreciate his tone—it was rude and dismissive. It made me think that I had been so wrong about him.

"Your girlfriend," I said.

Of course he had a girlfriend. He was gorgeous, and I'd seen all the girls' heads turn when we were walking around the city.

"I don't have a girlfriend."

"Ladies and gentlemen, take your seats." The man who I assumed was the professor came in looking very scholarly in his tweed jacket and slacks. In my head, I envisioned him in a leather chair, sucking at the end of a pipe.

I took the first seat by me, but Pierce slid two seats over, grabbing his bag from the seat next to me. Okay then. Tears welled in my eyes, but I sucked them back. How could I have been so wrong about him?

The professor didn't waste any time. "I'm Professor Jorgensen, and welcome to Principles of Marketing. If you're not supposed to be in this class, then find your way out."

No one left.

"Okay then. Along with me, you get the assistance of a teacher's assistant this year. Stand up, Mr. Wainwright." He signaled in Pierce's direction, and I turned my head to look behind Pierce, but Pierce was the one who stood.

What the hell?

He turned and waved to the class, completely avoiding looking at me.

"Believe me, he will be easier on you than me, so you should look forward to his lectures. Now let's get started..."

The rest of the class was a blur. I didn't know what to do or how to act, and I didn't feel Pierce's eyes on me once.

I waited patiently for class to end, but as soon as the professor let us go, Pierce grabbed his bag and left with the professor, leaving me no chance to ask any more questions.

"And what happened at dinner?" Kenzie asks, eyes wide.

I shake my head. "There was no dinner."

"Why not?"

"I texted him, but he never texted me back. Ever. He ignored me for the first month, then kept challenging me the rest of the semester. Poking holes and questioning every one of my responses. We'd go back and forth, and it just felt like he was trying to embarrass me. I was so hurt and broken that I'd put my blind faith in someone, and he just tossed me aside like I was nothing. Wouldn't even give me the respect of a conversation. Mortification mixed with shame, and I dreaded going to that class the entire semester. I mean, we weren't in love. It was one weekend, but it really felt like the start of something and... I don't know."

"You don't have to justify what you felt. Your feelings are valid, and right now I want to stomp out of here, up that mountain, and push him off a cliff." Tessa goes to the cupboard and takes a Christmas cookie out of the tin someone must have brought.

"But she's just going to drown her anger in sugar instead." Kenzie laughs.

"I should tell your brother. That's what I should do." Tessa points the cookie at us, making her way back over to the couch. Before she reaches it, she stops, goes back, swipes the tin off the counter, and comes back, setting it in her lap.

"You're not telling anyone. It was six years ago. Look at me. I'm doing great." I hold out my arms.

Kenzie quirks an eyebrow.

"What?" My forehead wrinkles.

"You're not the easy-going, smart-mouthed Brynn I'm used to. Him being here is affecting you, so tell us what you're thinking." Kenzie jabs me with a question I'm not ready to answer.

"Give me some time to get over the fact that I'm sharing a villa, my holiday, and my family with him this year. I don't know... part of me thinks that maybe it feels unfinished because I never got to say goodbye. I didn't attend the final class because my grandpa was having surgery."

"I guess that could be it," Tessa says with a frown.

"Or maybe it's just that I need to process the fact that he wants a second chance with me. Said he wants me back."

"Aww..." Kenzie says, her hand over her heart.

Tessa scowls at her best friend. "Not aww... try asshole."

I raise my hand at Tessa. "I love this whole older sister protective vibe you got going on, but that might be a bit much."

"So, you've forgiven him?" Tessa asks.

"I don't know. I think I'm grown up enough to understand why he backed away, even if he did handle it terribly, but that doesn't mean I'm ready to trust that he won't hurt me again."

They nod.

"Understandable," Tessa says.

Kenzie places her hand on my knee. "Just don't miss the opportunity. I mean." She glances at Tessa and puts her hand up to her as if that's going to keep Tessa from saying anything. "He clearly still affects you, and I see how you look at him sometimes."

"I do not."

She gives me an expression asking if I really want to argue about this.

"Ugh," I say and let my head flop back into the couch cushion.

"It was six years ago, and you were both younger, in a time of your life where your future was in limbo. I'm sure you've both grown up a lot since that time."

Why did I stay back to talk to them?

"If he hurts you again, he can expect some TNT," Tessa says.

Kenzie rolls her eyes.

"TNT?" I arch an eyebrow.

"Tre and Tessa. We're explosive together." She pretends she's punching the air. I do love our sisterly bond.

"In the bedroom, Tessa," Kenzie says.

"That is true."

They laugh, and I pretend to cover my ears.

Kenzie's words float around in my head, but I'm not ready to absorb them just yet. I guess time will tell. We're stuck together for the next seven days, so I have time to figure it out.

I like Tre and Carter, but I'm thankful to have a little alone time with my cousin. Since Tre and Carter are snowboarders like their sister, and Andrew and I are skiers, we decided to head up on the lift together to try out a different run.

"So, what is going on?" Andrew asks as soon as we're alone.

I stare at the skiers working their way down the mountain underneath us.

"Come on. Tell me what happened."

"It's a long story."

"Then let's head down the hill and get a drink at the lodge."

I'm not sure when Andrew got in touch with his feelings, though I'm sure it has something to do with the small blonde he's married to. The same one who has made him love Christmas again.

"That's okay. I can handle my shit."

"Pierce. I know since I moved here that we're not as close, but what's going on? First, you're not teaching anymore, and you want to leave London which isn't something you ever entertained before."

The wind whips around us and a dusting of snow hits my face.

I groan. "I feel like I'm going through a midlife crisis, and I'm only thirty."

"Okay, let's start by dealing with the most pressing dilemma—Brynn."

Just her name spurs a bolt of electricity to flow through my veins. I wanted to ski with her today in the hopes that we could connect a little more. But maybe since we're teamed up for the Russell family contest, it will give me more time alone with her.

"Six years ago, she did a semester abroad, and we met at a pub, spent the weekend together, and found out on Monday morning that I was her teacher's assistant. End of story." The lift is coming to the end, and I get ready to hop off.

"If that's the end of the story, then how come every time she comes near you, you can't stop looking at her?"

I shrug, trying to play it off. "She's hot, you can't deny that."

Brynn holds that beauty that makes me amazed there's not a line of guys following her around, hoping to get their chance with her.

"I'm married, so I can't comment on that."

"I'm sure Kenzie is the only one you see."

"She is."

I smirk, and we both get off the lift, stopping once we're a good distance away.

"Let's just ski and have fun. It's been a long time since we've spent any time together."

He nods, but I know he's going to drill me later on this topic. "Just do me a favor? Don't pursue her if you're not serious. I really like the Russells, and they're like Kenzie's second family. I don't want them to hate me because my cousin fucked with their daughter's head."

My shoulders fall. "I can't guarantee you where it might go. We barely started off last time. And I'm not sure she'll give me a chance anyway. But I've always wondered what could have been with us. She's the woman who always infiltrates my thoughts whenever I date someone else. I think that means something, and I want to see who we could be as a couple."

He nods and pats my shoulder. "Okay. Just wanted to make sure."

"I'd never do that to you. I'm sure if all I wanted was sex, I could find that on the hills."

Just as I say that, three women ski by, all of them looking over their shoulder at Andrew and me. Neither of us pay them any attention except to wait for them to start their descent before we head to the top of the hill.

* * *

At lunchtime, Andrew decides to go back to the villa and check on Kenzie and Nolan. I decide to stay at the lodge to have lunch there and away from everyone. I'm not by myself for long because Carter and Faith show up and decide that since it's busy, they'll join my table instead of waiting for one of their own.

Wonderful.

"What are you eating?" Carter glances at my plate.

"Chicken salad."

"Oh, I need something warm," Faith says and exaggerates a shiver. "Do you think they have soup bowls? Like the ones in bread?"

Faith seems like a nice person, but she seems a little checked out sometimes. It surprises me that she's with Carter because he said he's an IT guy, and from my experience, IT

PIPER RAYNE

guys aren't really into having to explain things. They always talk to you as though you're an idiot when you don't understand something.

"Yeah, a bread bowl." Carter laughs and kisses her cheek. "You're so cute."

I'm fairly certain that if I ever called Brynn cute in a condescending tone like that, she'd knee me in the bullocks.

"I think they had chili and a chicken and rice soup or something," I say.

After the big breakfast this morning, I needed something lighter, but I was still hungry after skiing most of this morning. I lean back and sip my fizzy pop, staring at the mountains.

"Faith!" a woman shouts across the lodge.

Carter looks over my shoulder then looks back at Faith. "Did you tell her we were coming here?"

Faith shrugs. "I just said we were getting something to eat."

Carter looks at me. "This woman has clung to Faith since our second run this morning."

"I think she felt bad for me. She said she learned to ski last year, saw me kind of struggling, and gave me some tips."

Carter blows out an aggravated breath.

"Do you mind if I join you?" The woman is already pulling out the fourth chair at our table before any of us have a chance to answer. "It's crazy busy in here." The redhead looks around the table. "Oh, hi. Who are you?" she asks me as if *I'm* the outsider.

Which I am in part, but I've known Carter and Faith longer than this woman.

"Pierce," I say.

"O.M.G. Is that a British accent?"

Bloody hell. I have a feeling Carter doesn't need to be upset about all the time this woman is spending with Faith because I'm about to be her new fascination. This happens

102

from time to time when I travel outside of the United Kingdom. She's probably going to ask me to say certain words just to hear my accent.

"I'm Kacey," she says, putting out her hand.

I shake it and return mine to my glass.

"Kacey is here with her family, but none of them are big skiers." Carter raises his eyebrows.

"Yeah. I was so happy when I found Faith and Carter." She smiles and raises her hand at the waitress who's just walking past after helping another table. "Excuse me."

The waitress looks at me. She wasn't all that friendly taking my order, so this should really make her day. "I thought you were alone," she deadpans, her gaze solely on me.

"They just joined." I shrug.

Her eyes scour the area. "You'll have to give me about five." She goes to walk away, but Kacey grabs her wrist.

"No boundaries," Carter mumbles.

The waitress strips her hand out of Kacey's hold. "Excuse me?"

"I just need a water. I'm so dehydrated," she whines.

Carter grunts, staring at Faith with annoyance. I'm with him on this.

I reach behind me to grab my wallet, so I can pay and get out of here, when Carter raises his hand. "Brynn!"

I stop reaching for my wallet, but Kacey takes that opportunity to grab my hand. This woman has no idea about personal space.

Carter's hand lowers, and his smile widens for his sister.

"I was supposed to meet Mom and Dad here." Her eyes fall to Kacey's hand on mine.

"Oh, hi," she says, shaking her head and concentrating on Carter.

I slide my hand out from under Kacey's.

"Who are you?" Kacey asks.

Carter laughs and crosses his arms as though he's ready for the show to begin.

"Who are you?" Brynn asks, arching a brow.

"I'm Kacey."

Brynn glances at me then back at Kacey. "I'm Brynn."

"Hi, Brynn. Am I missing something?" Kacey looks at Faith. "Is that his girl?"

"Why don't you ask me?" Brynn crosses her arms, and this is the first time I see the brother/sister resemblance between her and Carter.

"You're not British."

Brynn looks at me. I hold up my hands, wanting to see this play out because I think there might be jealousy running through Brynn's veins, and I like it. A lot. Though she's got nothing to worry about.

Brynn juts out her hip and glares at Kacey. "I don't have to be British for him to be mine, but to be clear, he's not. So, go ahead, Kacey, take your best shot." She turns to Carter, but I swing my arm around Brynn's waist and tug her onto my lap.

I am not going to let this Kacey think she has a chance with me.

"She's just joking, I'm hers, and she's mine."

"Ohhh..." Faith says and playfully slaps Carter's arm.

I'm pretty sure when it comes to overprotective brothers, Tre is the bigger concern. But Carter probably thinks I'm doing this to get Kacey to go find her family and to not let her think she has a shot with me.

"Pierce," Brynn says, but she doesn't move off my lap.

"I'm sorry," Kacey says, and the tension in Brynn's body lessens with the vulnerable tone in Kacey's voice. "I didn't mean... I'm just lonely. You know, it's the holidays, and it's like a big billboard-sized reminder that you don't have someone special to share it with. And..."

"We get it, Kacey." Faith smiles at her.

"How about I loan you Pierce for a little bit while I go snowboarding?" Brynn jumps off my lap, but I follow her, reaching for my wallet and tossing down money.

"I'm going to join you, honey. I missed you this morning."

"Oh, sweetie, you'll never keep up with me." She gives me a saccharine smile.

I turn to Kacey. "She's kind of competitive."

"Kind of? Just wait." Carter rolls his eyes.

"See you guys later." I wave, but Brynn is already halfway through the lodge by the time I catch up to her.

"You owe me," she says once we're outside.

"For what?"

"For getting you out of an afternoon with Kacey."

"Are you sure you didn't enjoy it a little bit?"

She crosses her arms. "Enjoy what?"

"You were a little bit jealous." I put my fingers in the air with some space between my thumb and forefinger.

"Please." She pretends to laugh as if it's an absurd idea.

"Come on. Tell me."

Her fingers wrap around mine, and she shrinks the open space, pressing my thumb and finger closer together. "Maybe that amount."

"I knew it."

She turns and walks toward the slopes.

I laugh, following her. I'm thankful I read that one right, otherwise it would have been terribly embarrassing.

She's warming up to me, and that's all I need.

Chapter Sixteen

PIERCE

After we all finish dinner, and Nolan and Ryah are in their pajamas and ready for bed, the Russells start the competition.

"Everyone has a tree in their villa. And a box of craft supplies. You have a half hour to figure out what your plan is, and two hours to execute and decorate your trees. Themes are encouraged. At two hours, pictures will be taken and posted for people to vote." Gwen is so hyped up, I'm surprised she doesn't have a whistle and stopwatch.

"Who is voting?" I ask, and everyone laughs.

"Mom's Facebook friends," Tre says.

"Pretty much the whole town of Climax Cove," Carter adds.

"And just so you know, they aren't always kind." Brynn laughs along with her brothers.

Their bond is tight, and I wonder what it's like to grow up with siblings. I had friendships in boarding school, but to have someone you grew up in the same house with who shares your blood is different.

Andrew and I share a look. He has to admit this is unusual

even for him, although he appears to be eating it up with a ladle.

"Go!" Gwen shouts, and Brynn pulls me by the sleeve of my sweater toward a corner.

My eyes follow everyone else, seeing each twosome find their own private space.

"Okay, let's think of a theme. Holiday movies?" Brynn taps the pen to her lips, and I get distracted for a moment. "*The Grinch... Christmas Vacation...* ugh... why am I drawing a blank?"

She's got me on holiday movies. I haven't seen any unless I was forced to.

"*Rudolph... Home Alone... White Christmas*, but that would be boring. Any ideas, marketing man?"

"I haven't seen a lot of Christmas movies."

Her mouth opens, and she stares at me. "What do you watch in December?" There's a look on her face as if she's genuinely concerned for me.

"I don't know." I shrug. "But we could do a Christmas-type theme instead of a movie."

"Like..." She waves.

"I just want to put the disclaimer out there that it's not fair that two marketing gurus are a team!" Carter shouts from somewhere behind me.

Brynn shakes her head and pays him no attention.

"We could do a song? 'Jingle Bells'... or the 'Twelve Days of Christmas'... what about that bloody song, 'Santa Claus is Coming to Town'?"

She's nodding, contemplating my ideas. "I love 'Twelve Days of Christmas,' but do we have time to make all the ornaments? And they're intricate. Like, how are we going to cut out a bunch of lords a-leaping?"

"Or maids a-milking?"

She laughs, and I love that I spurred that out of her.

"Okay, next idea." She taps the pen on her lips again. "Oh! Have you ever seen the movie, *Elf*?"

I shake my head, and she groans.

"Would you be okay if I took the lead?"

"Just direct me what to do. But can you explain the movie to me?"

She nods and scoots closer so our knees touch. "He's a guy who believed he was an elf and lived in the North Pole. When he was a baby, he snuck into Santa's sack..." She tells me the whole story, and when she's midway through, it starts to sound familiar.

"Is this a Will Ferrell movie?"

She nods, smiling. "You've seen it?"

"Bits and pieces, but I know the green-and-yellow outfit."

"Perfect." She puts pen to paper. "So, we'll make little elves, and maple syrup was really big in the movie, so we'll cut some of those. Candy canes and snowballs too. Actually no..."

Watching her mind work and spin the ideas to fruition is something I could do all night. The way she taps her pen, scribbles, and scratches out things. She's not shy about throwing any idea out there, and I fall for her a little more during this brainstorming session.

"Everyone ready?" Gwen calls.

That half hour went way too fast.

"Go to your villas, and in two hours, you have to be standing outside your villa door."

"The rules are somewhat strict, aren't they?" I say to Brynn as we rush to our villa.

"We take it seriously," she says without a glance behind her.

I catch up, but she slips on a piece of ice and falls back. My arms stretch out to catch her, but my foot catches the same piece of ice, and we both go down. The only thing I can do is maneuver us off the cement and onto a pile of snow.

"Perfect! The power couple is down. Hurry, everyone!" Carter shouts, laughing maniacally as he and Faith enter the villa next to ours.

"You okay?" I ask, but she scurries to her feet.

"We're on the clock!" Brynn recovers quickly while I'm lying on the ground, relishing that I had her in my arms again.

I get up and follow her inside.

She's already going through the construction paper, pulling out all the green and yellow. "Do you think you can do the maple syrup bottles? I can do the Buddies."

"Yeah." I nod.

"Perfect."

I'd hoped for the two of us to have time for some conversation while we're alone, wanted to take the opportunity to win her over a little. But she's way too distracted by the contest for me to make any headway. Maybe that's by design.

* * *

An hour later, our floor and coffee table look like a nursery school room, but the tree is coming together. Brynn's drawing faces on the Buddy characters, while I make the garland. We still have the candy canes and stacks of snowballs to complete.

"You're a genius," I say because I never would have come up with something like this. I would have researched before deciding what I was going to do.

"No." She shakes her head, concentrating on adding the faces with her marker.

"You know that in class, I called on you a lot to hear your theories. They were never standard. You have a gift for brand marketing." I tape the rings of paper garland together, which is hard to do with my large fingers. But Brynn said everyone else in her family would do rings of colored garland like they used to make in grade school and insisted I do it this way.

"I do enjoy it. Figuring out the audience, the way to bring awareness. And when it succeeds, it's kind of a high to try to do it again, you know?" Her eyes rise to meet mine.

I shake my head. "I don't. I've only really ever taught it."

She doesn't say anything at first, and I think maybe the conversation is going to end. "Why do you want to leave teaching?"

"I feel like a fraud." It's the first time I've admitted it to anyone. It's been about two years since I wanted to see if all my knowledge would carry out into the real world.

"Fraud?"

Thankfully, she doesn't look up at me. I don't want to be so vulnerable in front of her, so it's easier if we can pretend to be busy. I continue to cut the garland.

"It's admirable, you know? The way you and other students go into the workforce and put the principles to work. I'm sure it twists and reforms how to go into the next project. I'm retelling other people's hypotheses and successes and failures."

She drops the marker and leans back against the couch. "I can see that, but you always had a different spin on the material when you taught our lessons."

Our eyes meet, and for a moment, I'm scared of what she's going to say. She picks up her marker and goes back to drawing the faces.

"I looked forward to your lectures. Just so you know."

I bite down my smile. "Well, I am a good-looking guy."

She looks up through her dark eyelashes at me, her hand still wrapped around her marker. "That wasn't the only reason." She smiles, and it pierces my heart like a dart hitting the bull's-eye.

I'd do just about anything to be able to push all this construction paper away, lower her to the carpet, and kiss her until her lips are bruised.

She gets up off the floor and sets the little Buddies together in a pile. "We better get working before the time runs out."

For the last hour, we only converse about the tasks we're completing and the overall look of the tree. Working alongside her is oddly peaceful, and the mutual respect we seem to give each other when we have an idea is encouraging. She even used my idea to have the garland come down the tree from the top rather than wrapping it around.

At the two-hour mark, we step outside, along with everyone else. They decide to start on the other side of the villas, leaving ours for last.

Andrew and Kenzie did a Santa Claus theme, making the tree an actual Santa. I'm actually surprised Andrew pulled it off, and I assume Kenzie did the majority of it since party planning is her thing. They might be our biggest competition.

Tre and Tessa's theme was white Christmas, which was beautiful with all the intricate snowflakes they made.

Abe and Gwen decorated theirs as a snowman with a giant top hat as a tree topper.

Carter and Faith's looked like a bunch of children decorated it.

Brynn nudges my arm and nods toward the big rings of multicolored construction paper wrapped around Carter's tree as a garland. It's nice to have an inside joke with her, I can't lie.

Gwen takes the pictures, then we all head back to the main house for some hot cocoa and a movie. It seems that everything is planned up to the minute, and I wonder if I'll ever get any alone time with Brynn.

"Random selections were made before we came here so there are no fights." Abe holds up a piece of paper and tapes it to the wall by the television.

"What's that?" I ask Brynn, who, surprisingly, has sat next to me.

"It's the Christmas movie list. Get ready because this week you're getting your fix of holiday movies whether you want to or not."

"Every year, a list is made, and we cross them off as we watch them," Tre says, holding a sleeping Ryah to his chest.

Gwen sits in the chair next to me, sipping her cocoa. "When these three were young, they'd spend days in front of the television arguing about what Christmas movie to watch."

"And I always got outvoted." Brynn glares at Carter. "How many times did I have to watch *Bad Santa*?"

"Which was inappropriate." Abe glares at his sons while everyone else laughs.

"Well, it's not on this year's list," Gwen says.

Tre and Carter groan and share a look.

Brynn pulls a blanket from the back of the couch and lays it over her lap. "Press Play."

Someone dims the lights, and the television glows in front of us.

When the opening scene comes on, everyone but me shouts, "*Christmas Vacation*!"

Then they all point at one another and argue about who said it first.

When Andrew said they were competitive, I had no idea how much.

I'm starting to like it and them. Which is probably a good thing, because if I want to have a chance with Brynn, I need to want them to be part of our lives. They're all clearly close to one another, and they mean a lot to her.

Family.

Still a concept I have a hard time comprehending.

Chapter Seventeen

BRYNN

O nce again, I wake up to an empty villa.

It's like *Groundhog Day*—the bed is put away, the blankets and pillow neatly stacked on the end of the couch.

The only new thing is our decorated tree. I know we're going to earn the win today. The other trees were adorable in their own right, but ours is out of their league.

I pull on a sweatshirt, slide into my boots, and trek across the paved path to the main lodge, careful not to slip like I did last night. As soon as I open the door, I hear my mom's laugh.

I figured Pierce was working out, but he's in the kitchen with my mom, the two of them moving around one another as if they've done it for years.

Mom catches sight of me in the doorway. "Good morning, sleepyhead."

There's no one else in the villa, so I don't understand how I could be the last one awake.

"Where is everyone, and what are you two doing?" I rub the sleep from my eyes and reposition my ponytail. I thought I had time to make myself presentable, since yesterday the guys didn't come back from working out until much later.

"Everyone is relaxing in their villas, I suppose. Your dad had to run out to get more eggs."

I slide up onto the breakfast stool. "You're not working out this morning?" I ask Pierce, who is mixing up pancake batter.

"I'm a little sore from yesterday. I'm used to standing at a podium the majority of the day."

"What's it like being a professor?" Mom asks while I climb off the stool to get my coffee.

"I'll get it." Pierce stops me with a hand placed over mine on the counter. My gaze lifts to his, and he gives me a sweet smile.

"I got it." I slide my hand from under his and walk over to the beverage bar. I pour coffee from the carafe and add my milk and cinnamon as Pierce tells my mom about teaching at the university.

"I was just talking to Brynn about it last night. I enjoy it, but I think I want to do more than just teach about it now, and I figure I'm only getting older."

"How old are you?" she asks, pretending to be less interested than I know she is while she cuts up fruit for her yogurt parfait bar that's a staple in this family.

"Careful, Pierce, she's got her shovel," I say before sipping my coffee, walking back to the stool.

"Oh, stop it, Brynn. I'm getting to know our guest," she says innocently.

"I'm thirty," he answers.

If he was smart, he'd have waited to see if she was going to ask again.

"That's not too much older, right, Brynn?" She looks at me, reaching for a bag of granola.

"Too old for what, Mom?" We both know what she's implying.

"To start a new career," she says, winking at me.

Oh, Mom, stop matchmaking.

"That's why I was interviewing at the same place as Brynn."

The bag slips from my mom's grasp, and granola pours over the counter. "Oh crap."

I slide off the stool to help her clean up. Pierce stops measuring the pancake mixture to help too.

"Sorry, I'm a little clumsy this morning. I actually forgot that the two of you were going after the same job." She finishes with the granola while Pierce and I scoop up the pieces that fell and walk over to the trash can at the same time.

Life isn't fair. His hair looks just fucked, and I can't help but wish I was the reason it looked like that. No, I don't. What am I thinking?

"Well, Pierce is going to get it," I say, turning away from him and closing my eyes to get the ache between my thighs to dissolve.

"I don't think so. Your accomplishments in the workplace are impressive." Pierce takes the whisk, and his forearms flex with the movement of stirring the batter. Corded muscles, deep veins. God help me, I'm describing his forearm as if it's his dick.

"Maybe there's room for both of you?" my mom asks.

I laugh and shake my head. "Doubtful."

Thankfully, she lets the topic go and doesn't ask any further questions.

"Are you going to hit the runs today?" Pierce asks me.

"I'm not sure. I might scratch another movie off the list."

"You can watch movies after vacation. The two of you should be out there on the mountains." Mom arranges the yogurt parfait bar on the butcher block behind the table. She goes back and forth to make sure there are bowls and spoons.

"I'd love to go with you," Pierce says, turning on the burner and plopping butter on the griddle.

"Where did you learn to cook?" I ask, surprised by his skills. He doesn't seem like the type.

He looks out of the corner of his eyes at my mom, then back at the pancakes. "Um... boarding school."

My mouth falls open. "You went to boarding school?"

He nods and spoons the batter onto the hot griddle.

Mom is obviously intrigued because she leans her hip along the counter. "From what age?"

"Eleven to eighteen."

I'm not sure how comfortable he is talking about it, based on his body language. He's more closed off than I've ever seen him.

"Oh... did you enjoy it?" my mom asks.

"Mom," I say, giving her a look to say stop asking questions.

"It's okay." He picks up the spatula and stands straight, looking from my mom to me. "My parents died when I was eleven, so..."

I feel my mom's eyes on me, but I can't look away from Pierce. "I'm sorry," I whisper.

He shrugs. "It was a long time ago. In their will, they asked for Andrew's parents to be my guardians but wanted me sent to boarding school. Andrew's dad wanted to respect his brother's wishes, and so he did."

He studies the pancakes, flipping each one, and I take the moment to look at my mom.

There are tears in her eyes, but she doesn't let them fall, placing her hand on Pierce's shoulder. "I'm sorry to hear about your parents. They'd be proud of the man you've turned out to be. I mean, I know I don't know you very well, but from what I do know, you're a good man."

"Thank you, Gwen. Like I said, it was a long time ago... anyway, everyone had to work in the kitchen at some point, so I learned a lot." He nods and takes the pancakes off the griddle.

The door opens, and my dad stands there, holding bags full of groceries.

"Let me help you," I say, rushing off the stool before anyone else gets a chance.

"Thanks," Dad says. "What's going on in here? You all look like you're at a funeral."

"Oh god." I squeeze my eyes shut.

"Abe," my mom says with annoyance and takes a bag from me.

"What did I say?" He sets the other bags on the counter and unpacks them.

"I just told them that my parents died when I was eleven." Pierce says it so nonchalantly, as if it wasn't devastating.

My dad frowns. "I'm sorry to hear that."

"Like I said, it was a long time ago."

Pierce keeps saying that same thing, but can time really change the fact that you lost your parents at such a young age? That has to leave scars. I understand that you can get used to living alone, but it just confirms what I already feared— Andrew is Pierce's only family.

I can't imagine not having the support system of my parents and siblings. What must that feel like? And then your parents ask for you to go to boarding school to live with a bunch of strangers in the midst of your grief?

My dad doesn't ask any other questions. "Those pancakes look good," he remarks, walking by the stovetop and putting something in the cupboard.

"Abe, can you see if Carter and Faith are back while I go

see about the other ones? I don't want breakfast to get cold." Mom leaves the lodge.

"I just saw them get back from somewhere, so I'll knock and let them know." Dad follows my mom out the door, leaving me alone with Pierce.

Neither of us says anything, and I watch him.

"Please don't look at me like that," he whispers, pouring a new round of pancakes onto the griddle.

"I'm not." I shake my head, but I know that's why my parents left. To compose themselves.

"You are. I'm fine. I'm in one piece, living my life."

"Pierce..."

He finally glances up. "This is why I hate telling people. I hate that look on your face right now."

I walk around the island, unsure of my actions, but I'm going on gut instinct because it's what I would want if I was him. I wrap my arms around his waist and lean my head on his back. It rises and falls with a deep breath. He doesn't turn around or place his hands over mine on his stomach. But most of all, he doesn't push me away.

My heart would break for anyone who went through what he did, but I can't ignore the extra layers his story dug through me because I do care about him. No matter how much I push away these feelings for him, they're there.

The door opens, and I quickly unwrap my arms from around his waist, wiping my eyes and opening the fridge to pretend I'm looking for something.

"Yogurt parfait. Tessa's favorite." Tre comes in with Ryah in his arms.

She'll be a good distraction from the puzzling emotions for Pierce I can't piece together yet.

Chapter Eighteen

PIERCE

Andrew and I are sitting outside by the firepit, the smoke drifting toward the other side of the ring of chairs from where we sit.

Brynn and I won the tree decorating contest, so we're up on the board. I don't really care about that, but it put a perma-smile on Brynn's face, so that's a good thing.

"I told Brynn and Gwen... about my parents," I say, tapping my finger on my boot.

"Brynn didn't know?" Andrew asks.

"I didn't think it was a proper come-on line. 'My parents died when I was eleven, and instead of letting me go live with my aunt, uncle, and cousin, I had to go live at a boarding school.' It would have been like waving a red flag in her face."

He sips his beer and stares into the fire. "What did they say?"

What feels like a century ago, Andrew and I talked about the fact I was put in boarding school. He felt guilty for his dad's decision, but it wasn't on him. I don't even blame my uncle. I gave up a long time ago trying to understand why my parents wanted my uncle to use all the money they had to send me away from everyone who loved me, but then again, I feel as if I didn't even know my parents that well. On my twenty-third birthday, I realized that I had lived my life without my parents longer than I had with them, and it was a tough realization.

"I think Gwen was about to cry, but I did score a hug from Brynn." My attempt at humor dies because Andrew knows me too well, and he won't let me get away with it. "Come on, mate, I got a hug."

His lips tip up into a smile. "I'm pretty sure you want more than a hug."

He's not wrong.

"Am I crazy for thinking it could become something after all this time?" I ask. I want to push harder, but I'm scared that too much, too soon, and I'll end up pushing her further away.

"Who am I to say? I fell in love with an elf."

I laugh because his and Kenzie's first meeting was a funny one.

"In all seriousness, love sneaks up on you. It definitely wasn't love at first sight with Kenzie and me, but soon I wanted to spend every minute I had with her and like turned into something stronger. But it was different for me. I was scared to put myself out there. Correct me if I'm wrong, but this is your first time, right?"

I scowl at him. "I'm not a virgin." I use humor to deflect again because as much as I'm owning this rush of new emotions toward Brynn, I'm worried about addressing what that might mean for my future. "I never had anyone I felt like I could fall in love with, no."

He nods. "I thought so."

"Honestly, that whole sneaking up on you thing makes sense. I thought I was taking a hot girl home to screw her and then she'd bugger off. But afterward, I wanted her to stay the night, and the next morning, I wanted more time with her. I spent that entire semester with her in my class in a constant battle in my head—break the rules, date her in secret... but I was a coward."

"You were thinking of your future career."

I nod, tipping back my beer. "It might end up being my biggest regret."

"Mate, she was young. It might not have worked back then. She needed to go off and live some of her life."

Andrew's right, I know. But I didn't have to handle it the way I did. My bigger concern is whether I ruined it for us completely.

My gaze floats up from the fire to the windows of the main house. Brynn is dancing with Ryah in her arms, her niece's infectious smile on display. I imagine coming home after a day at work and seeing this exact image but with our own daughter.

"What about the job thing?" Andrew brings me back to the present.

"I'm not sure. I don't even know how many more applicants there are. I have a few leads in London too."

"Really?" Andrew sighs. "I had hopes of getting you closer to me."

I'm not sure what my life would look like without Andrew. He's kept in touch with me over the years and pushed our friendship when I didn't want anything to do with our family.

The younger, more delinquent version of me resented Andrew for growing up with a family and hated his father for putting me in boarding school. But as I grew, I matured and realized they weren't to blame. No one was really. It was just a shite situation that life handed us.

"We'll see what happens, but getting the job over Brynn would be a miracle. I did some research on her company in Portland, and she's done amazing work there."

He chuckles. "You sound like a proud dad."

I shake my head. "No, I just see her talent. I did when she was in my class too, so I'm not surprised. I'm envious, honestly."

We don't say anything for a few minutes, just stare at the flames licking the cold night air.

Kenzie pops her head out the door. "Sorry, guys, but it's time."

"She really pushes you out of your comfort zone." I down the rest of my beer and stand.

"Yeah, you'd probably pass out if I told you the stuff she's made me do, but it makes her happy, and her happiness makes me happy. She pushes me to be a better man too." He clasps his hand on my shoulder. "Do me a favor? Follow your heart and don't listen to the doubts, okay? They're a waste of time, and they're usually not right anyway."

I nod, but it's not as easy as he makes it sound.

All of this is new to me. The family, the feelings, but most of all the desire—the fact that I want these things when I was happily living my life without them.

* * *

"All right, I'm going to hand out the cookies, and when you're done decorating, we'll take pictures for the Facebook friends to vote. Usually we do the prettiest cookie, but we're going to mix it up this year, since some of us aren't as artistic as others."

Tre coughs out, "Carter."

"Don't call me next time you need computer advice." Carter gives him the finger.

"Don't worry, I know how to turn off my computer and turn it back on," Tre jokes.

Carter throws a marshmallow from the bowl, and it

bounces off Tre's forehead. Tre picks up sprinkles and throws them at Carter.

"You'll be cleaning it up," Gwen says, placing a cookie in front of Brynn. "These are ugly sweaters. Decorate your cookie like the ugliest sweater, and we'll see who wins."

She sets one cookie each on the plate between the team members as though she's our teacher, and we're all in primary school. She and Abe sit at the head of the table.

"You have a half hour. Go," Abe says.

Everyone scatters, reaching for icing, knocking elbows, and I sit back and watch the scene unfold. Brynn's got it handled for both of us.

"Do you have any ideas?" she asks once she's amassed all the supplies she wants.

I nod at the cookie. "Do your worst."

She smiles and lowers her attention to the cookie.

"You coming to the gym tomorrow, Pierce?" Tre asks. Most of the men in the partnerships aren't contributing to the cookie contest. Not even Abe.

"I think I overdid it with the workout and then skiing all day yesterday." I sit up and stretch my back the best I can. "The sofa bed isn't helping."

Brynn glances up from the corner of her eye but doesn't say anything.

"Come on, Brynn, you're all 'independent woman, hear me roar.' Why aren't you guys swapping every night?" Carter asks.

Brynn grabs a red cinnamon candy and throws it at him. It hits his eye.

"Damn it, my eye." He covers his eye.

Brynn looks at Tre, sharing some type of understanding I assume has something to do with Carter when they were growing up.

"I take it you won't be at the gym?" Tre asks Carter.

"I think Faith and I are sleeping in tomorrow. So, no wake-up calls."

Tre turns back to me, disregarding his brother who keeps blinking as if Brynn did permanent damage. "I like the stretching routine you do before you work out."

We continue to chat about how I like to stretch for a good twenty minutes before I work out to loosen everything up. Tre's pretty cool and doesn't bug me with questions or sexual innuendos about his sister and me, which is refreshing. I'm not sure how he'd be if we were actually dating though.

"Brynn, come with," Tre says.

"I'm on vacation." She doesn't look up from her cookie, making perfect squiggly lines across the sweater cookie.

"Well, you're not getting any other exercise if Pierce is on the sofa bed." Carter laughs. "Ouch. Fuck." He reaches down and rubs his leg.

"Language, we have little ears around," Gwen says, concentrating on her cookie just as much as her daughter.

Abe is with the kids in the corner area with the toys now. He's a great grandpa, always spending as much time with Ryah as he can.

"So, you're a baker?" I ask Tessa.

Tre puts his arm around his wife. "The best."

Gwen clears her throat but laughs after. No one else says anything, and I feel as if it's an inside joke I'm not part of.

"Actually, I got a call from my business partner today, Brynn. She thinks we need to work on getting more social awareness and wondered if when you got back to Portland, maybe you'd have some ideas. We'd pay you." Tessa puts down her icing, sits back, and slides the plate toward Tre. "Make it ugly for me while I pretend to ignore what you're doing."

Everyone laughs because her cookie has an ugly sweater, but the piping and decorations look too good to eat.

Tessa must notice me looking because she says, "Curse of the day job."

"You're very talented," I say.

"Isn't she?" Brynn says, sitting up and staring at her cookie as if she's inspecting it. "I'm super jealous of how artistic she is with sugar."

I put my arm around the back of Brynn's chair. "Everyone has their own talents. You're brilliant at making people want to buy something."

Her cheeks turn pink, and it feels good to pull a blush out of her.

When I look at the table though, Gwen, Tessa, and Tre are all staring at me with goofy smiles. I take those smiles to mean I'm making progress on my quest to win back Brynn.

Chapter Nineteen

P ierce and I head back to our villa after watching *Four Christmases*.

"I quite enjoyed that movie," he says.

I press in the code for the door and step inside, admiring our tree. I left it plugged in when we left earlier, so the lights on it fill the room with a warm glow.

"Tomorrow we have to be on our game. I'm pretty sure it's gingerbread house night because my mom will want to display them, then everyone will pick them apart to eat before Christmas."

"Want to sketch out some ideas?" he asks, walking past me toward the couch.

"You'd want to do that?"

"One thing I've figured out about you is how much you love to win, so if us winning the gingerbread house competition makes you happy, I'll grab my notebook."

I watch him reach into his bag next to the couch and bring a notebook to his lap. I sit down next to him and turn on the television. "Want to watch a movie while we do it?"

He looks at me, and his gaze falls to my lips. "Please don't get my hopes up like that."

"What?" I ask, and his gaze floats back up to meet mine.

"While we do it?" He smirks.

I push his shoulder, and he pretends to lose his balance, laughing. "Dirty mind."

"Only when it comes to you."

I'm not sure what to say, so I say nothing. After he told us this morning that he lost his parents so young and went to a boarding school, I had the urge to soothe any leftover pain, but when I hugged him, I got no reciprocation, so I took that as a sign it's still a sensitive matter.

"Thanks for helping my mom so much in the kitchen," I say, scrolling through the streaming channel to find a good holiday movie that Pierce might enjoy too.

"I like to cook. Clears my head." He opens the notebook. His legs are stretched out to rest his feet on the coffee table, his ankles crossed. "What are you thinking?"

I click on *Surviving Christmas* because it's one of my favorites, but I turn my body to face Pierce. "In the past, it's not really been about the houses but the stuff around the house."

"Like a front porch swing?" He glances up from the corner of his eye.

"What?" My head tilts.

Without responding to me, he sketches out a gingerbread house with a front porch that wraps around it and points the tip of his pen to where he thinks we could put the porch swing. "Here?"

"Pierce." My tone is questioning. Is he doing what I think he's doing?

He draws it in place. "I think this is a good spot. And a fence around the front of the yard, right? You wanted that too." He continues to draw a small picket fence with a swinging gate that opens from the sidewalk to a brick path up to the front door.

My heart rate picks up speed. "Pierce."

He pays me no attention and continues drawing the dream house I described to him our last night in bed together. It was so easy to tell him what I wanted in my life.

"A simple life, right? A marriage like your parents. A house with a front porch swing and fence in the front so you can watch your kids play? Oh wait." He presses the pen back to the paper. "A dog."

"Pierce..." My voice is a hoarse whisper now. I can't believe he remembered everything I told him.

"Is this about right?" he asks, holding it out to me as if he's an architect.

I have no words because it's perfect. "Yeah," I say, turning around and facing the television.

"Did you think I'd forget?" he asks, voice serious.

"Hoped maybe." I stare at my lap, my fingers fidgeting until I stuff my hands under my thighs.

"Why? I've thought about that conversation so many times. Wondered about the parents whose marriage you put high on a pedestal. Wondered if I could have had you think as highly of me as you thought of your dad. Most of all, could I have been the man who was lucky enough to give you that life?"

I stand, unsure where to go, but unable to sit here any longer. "You..." I take a deep breath. "You can't just say things like that."

"What am I doing? Recounting the time we had together."

I throw my hands in the air. "You told me nothing. All this does is confirm that I bared myself to you, and you told me nothing about yourself. The connection I've been chasing with every guy after you... it was all a fraud because you never even told me about your parents' death or that you went to boarding school or anything about your life now that I think about it."

He stands but doesn't approach me. "Because I didn't want that pitying look. Not from you. I didn't want that to factor into what you felt for me. You want to know what I figured out that first night we met?"

"Not really." I shake my head.

"That you had a huge heart, and you were one of those people who takes other people in. And now that I've met your family, I see it's been ingrained in you from birth. They're all welcoming and trying to help me be comfortable. So, let's say that on the first night I dumped my shitty past in your lap—it would have been the only thing you saw about me."

"You don't know that. You didn't give me a chance."

He breezes by me, grabs his coat off the coat rack, and shrugs it on before leaning closer, his lips so close to my ear. "I do know because when you found out, you hugged me so tightly that for the first time in years, tears filled my eyes. It made me feel weak, and that's not how I ever want you to see me." He turns and opens the door, leaving.

Twenty minutes go by and still no sign of Pierce. When a knock lands on the door, I open the door, thinking maybe he forgot the code. But of course it isn't him.

My mom stands in her pajamas, a coat wrapped around her. "I saw Pierce leave." I rush into her arms, and she wraps them around me, running her hands down my back. "Are you finally ready to talk to me?"

I nod into her down coat, and she nudges me inside so she can shut the door.

"Want to start from the beginning?" She goes over to the coffee pot and places a hot cocoa pod into the machine.

As it brews, I tell her our story. Him picking me up from the pub, the walk around London, his apartment, and me spending the weekend with him.

"I'm just not sure I want to go there again," I say.

She hands me a cup of cocoa and sits with her own on the couch. "Brynn, you've always had this fierceness about you. Smart-mouthed. Wanting to keep up with your brothers made you tough, and I never felt that I had to worry about you except for one thing." She nods toward my heart. "Your heart was always open, and I had a feeling when you came back from London that someone had hurt you. You didn't approach love as freely and with open arms like you had before. The longer you never brought anyone home, never talked about a man, it just cemented my assumption. Now that I've met the man who—"

"He didn't break my heart. I only knew him for a couple months, and it was over in one weekend." I sip my cocoa.

My mom stares at me. "He broke something. Maybe it was your ability to sink into that hope at the beginning of a relationship. Maybe it made you afraid of being hurt again." She sighs. "I blame your dad and me. We just showed you too good of a life." She laughs.

"Mom." I shake my head at her.

"I know. I know. But I think he was your first realization that life isn't always easy. Pierce might not have broken your heart, but maybe he crushed your spirit. He was young himself, though. And now that I know about his past, that's a lot of stuff to deal with for a young man."

"What am I supposed to do?"

"Do you still like him? Those butterflies zooming?"

I nod.

"After London, did you survive?"

I nod, pressing my lips together.

"If this doesn't work out, it will hurt, but you'll get

through it like you did last time. It's never a mistake to love someone who's worthy of it, should never be a regret to go all in. If it works out, there are no regrets, and the only way you'll ever know is to go for it. What if your future is filled with love?"

I rock my head back. My mom always gives the best talks, and this is exactly why I didn't want to go to her first. I knew she'd encourage me to give Pierce another chance. And it's scary. Whether it should be or not, it is.

"From what I've seen, he's mature and owns his past. He's comfortable with the man he's become. He's confident and respectful and knows the mistakes he made with you." She puts her cocoa on the table. "The way he looks at you, Brynn..."

I shake my head, wanting her to tell me but not at the same time.

"It's what I've always wanted for you. Just like when Tre brought Tessa home. Carter." She rocks her head back and forth. "We'll see what the future brings him."

We both laugh. I like Faith, but she gives in to him a lot.

"Thanks, Mom."

She scoots closer and hugs me. "Always. Don't waste time fighting it. Just see where it takes you. That's the entire point of life."

I nod as the door opens. Looking over my mom's shoulder, I see Pierce in the doorway, staring at us.

"It's him, isn't it?" my mom whispers.

"Yeah."

"You got this, and if it goes south, the whole family will support you until you can stand on your own again." She draws back. "And your brothers will kick his ass." Her eyes meet mine for a few seconds before I nod.

She stands. "Hello, Pierce." Then she glances at the television. "Brynn's favorite movie, *Surviving Christmas*. It's a good one. See you all in the morning." She puts her hand on Pierce's upper arm as she passes him.

His gaze is fixed on mine. My mom is right—why not just take the chance and hope it pays off in the end?

Chapter Twenty

BRYNN

My mom nudges Pierce into the villa and shuts the door.

"Hi," I say. "Where did you go?"

He takes off his jacket and boots, leaving both by the door. "I went for a walk, but it's really cold, so I didn't last that long."

"Hmm... that's kind of weak," I joke, and he raises his eyebrows. "Yeah, okay, bad timing." I pat the spot next to me. "Can we talk?"

He walks over and sits on the couch.

"I'm sorry," I say, unsure how to broach this subject. It seems very adult, and I'm not always good at serious matters.

"You don't have to apologize. It's my own issue, and I shouldn't lay it all on you." His eyes remain on the television.

"Can you look at me?"

He turns toward me. "It's fine, Brynn. I'm sorry for storming out or making you feel bad for trying to comfort me. Yours was a natural response."

"God, Pierce, want to think for me a little more?"

He rears his head back. "I'm telling you it's my fault."

"I was wrong."

You'd think I'd just told him I was pregnant with his baby with how confused he looks. "No."

"Yes, Pierce. When I saw you in that hotel, a huge part of me wanted to walk into your room, accept your invitation for a drink, but all the anger of being ignored those months rushed back and came out. I've been giving you the cold shoulder, but it was a protective seal, which I now realize because of my mom."

His face softens, and he twists his body to face me fully. "What are you saying?"

I swallow, glance at my lap, and back up. "I want to see what's between us."

"Meaning?"

"Meaning I want to give us another chance. I know we live in two different countries, and we're competing for the same job, but... oh, I don't know. I just think if I let this week go by, I'll regret that more than I would if it doesn't work out. Does that make sense?"

"Yeah, definitely." He scoots closer, and I see his hand rising toward my face.

"I'd like nothing more than to take you to that bed and put all the shit behind us right now, but I'm just not ready yet."

He draws back and nods. "Okay."

"I hope you're not disappointed."

"Never. Don't ever worry about disappointing me. I've waited six years, I'll wait until you're ready. Just tell me when."

I nod. "Would you settle for cuddling while we watch the movie?"

"Settle? Fuck, I've wanted you in my arms since I saw you in that elevator." He straightens and puts his feet on the table in front of him, placing his arm over the back of the couch, waiting for me.

I snuggle into his body, and damn, he smells so good. I lean in and inhale him. He chuckles, probably knowing exactly what I'm doing.

"I'm sorry for giving you a hard time about the hug. I'm an asshole when it comes to my past."

I shake my head. "The only thing I want to tell you is to not feel weak because of people wanting to comfort you. I hugged you because I care for you and wanted to ease the pain I saw on your face. Not because I felt bad for you."

He nods. "Thanks." His hand runs down my arm and back up.

We watch the movie, and yeah, it's my favorite, but there's a weight lifted off me that makes me enjoy it more than the other two I watched with my family.

* * *

The next evening, Mom says that Tre and Tessa won the cookie decorating contest with their ugly sweater. Carter insists it's because Tessa is a professional and Mom's friends were actually judging the best-looking cookie, not the worst.

That makes Pierce and me tied with Tre and Tessa, but there are still a lot of events to go.

I look at Pierce across the room when my mom announces that it's gingerbread house time.

Along the table, she sets down all different shapes and sizes of cooked gingerbread, saying we don't need to stick to the classic house if we don't want to. The problem is that if you're not fast enough, you're stuck making a structure that will be the ugliest house or unstable, like Tre and Tessa's last year.

I crack my neck and roll my shoulders as if I'm getting ready to run a marathon or something. Pierce laughs.

"No fighting, and no one leaves here until every sprinkle

is picked up. You've got three hours. Go!" Mom steps away from the table while we rush it, grabbing all the parts to a house.

Thankfully, Nolan and Ryah are asleep in their playpens, and they've proven that they can sleep through anything. Maybe because they're so exhausted from being off their schedules and all the fresh air. I don't know, but it works.

"Are we doing it like the sketch?" Pierce asks me.

"What sketch? Did you know we were doing this?" Carter points at me. "Cheaters!"

"Everyone knows Mom does the gingerbread house every year, so if you didn't already think about what you wanted to build, that's on you."

"She has a point, Carter. And it doesn't mean she can actually construct it." Tre's eyes lift in challenge, and I narrow mine.

I turn toward Pierce and nod. Our hands and arms are intertwined while we try to get the frosting to stick the gingerbread pieces together. I've never thought that decorating a gingerbread house could produce sexual tension, but we're so close, and we keep touching. I'm starting to get turned on. The scent of his musky cologne isn't helping. It makes me want to lean into his neck and inhale.

Hour by hour, I feel myself softening toward him. Maybe it's me keeping my guard up, but I'm not that wide-eyed, naïve girl he met six years ago. I want him to discover the woman I've become and make sure we're still a good fit before bringing sex into it and complicating things. Things being feelings.

Pierce makes a swing with licorice and pretzels, somehow getting it to adhere to the roof of the porch that wraps around our house.

"Damn, Wainwright, are you a structural engineer in your spare time?" Carter asks.

"My partner is pretty badass, huh?" I grin across the table at my brother.

Everyone stops and stares at me, then each other.

"Did you just compliment Pierce?" Tre asks.

"I can see people's good qualities," I say, making the brick path to the front door with Sweet Tarts.

"You haven't seen Pierce's since he arrived," Carter says. I kick him under the table. "Ouch. Seriously, I'm gonna have a bruise."

"Stop saying stupid shit," I say.

"Carter, can you do the roof?" Faith asks.

"Yeah, go be a productive partner to Faith and leave me alone." I shoo him away with my hand.

He does, but I think it's because he wants to get laid more than how much he actually wants to help. Whatever, it gets him out of my hair.

Three hours goes by in a blink, and we all hold up our sugar-coated fingers when Mom calls time.

I will say the couples with the kids kind of get the shaft. Andrew had to get Nolan once, and their house isn't the best as a result. Tre constructed the house and left it to Tessa to do most of the decorations while he kept Ryah occupied after she woke up. He's still so military despite having retired from it. Even in the way he assigns the tasks of the gingerbread house decorating.

Carter and Faith's house looks as though Ryah and Nolan put it together. Clearly this is not their forte.

Mom left most of it to Dad mostly because although his is only half-finished after three hours because he's a perfectionist, she knows it's his favorite contest. Couple goals.

My eyes veer to Pierce. He's watching me secretly judge everyone else's house. His smirk is sexy, and I have to clear my throat and look away. Now that I've opened myself up to allowing him in, I think he's grown more attractive overnight.

I watched him come off the hill today and could barely contain myself while he shrugged off his jacket. I'm in a lot of trouble.

Mom takes pictures of each team's gingerbread house, uploading them to Facebook for judging.

"And tonight's movie is...*The Holiday*," Mom announces once everything is clean.

"I'm going to head to our villa to give Ryah a bath. Hopefully she'll go down since she didn't sleep very long earlier," Tessa says. "You can stay here, Tre, I can handle it."

"No, let's go," Tre says, waving goodbye.

"Us too unfortunately," Kenzie says. "Nolan is so out of sorts. I need one good night of sleep from him if I'm going to make it to Christmas."

We say good night.

Carter hovers by the door. "Faith and I were going to go into town. And *The Holiday* isn't really my thing."

"Because it's more of a romance?" I ask.

"Yep." He places his hand on the small of Faith's back and urges her out the door.

"I guess it's just us four," Mom says.

"Yeah." *Awesome.*

This won't be uncomfortable at all.

My parents sit in chairs on either side of the couch, and I respectfully don't cuddle up to Pierce. That would be weird. I reach for the blanket as the movie starts.

"Do you mind sharing?" Pierce asks.

"Course not." I ignore my parents' side-eyes and lift it over his lap, causing me to scoot closer to him.

My knee touches his thigh, and who am I kidding? I have no idea how long I'll last before I grab him and smash my lips to his.

Halfway through the movie, my dad is snoring, and my mom's eyes are closed.

I pick up the remote and pause the movie. "Mom. Dad."

Both of them bolt up from their chairs.

"Sorry." Dad runs a hand down his face.

"You two go to bed. We'll close up the lodge," I say.

They both stand.

"Thanks, guys." My mom gives us a tired smile.

Dad puts his arm around my mom, and they make their way out the door.

Pierce lifts his arm, and I curl into his body, pressing Play on the movie. I run my hand along his muscled chest, slipping it under the hem of his sweatshirt. He doesn't say anything, and other than his fingers running down my arm and back, he continues to watch the movie.

My body buzzes. I want to lift myself and straddle him, feel how hard I make him. Why am I fighting this? I lift my lips to his neck, and he groans.

"What are you doing?" he whispers as if other people are in the room.

"I can't resist." I press my lips to his skin again, this time on his strong jaw.

He turns his head, and through the flicker of light from the movie, our eyes meet. "What do you want, Brynn?"

"I want you to kiss me."

He lowers his head and closes his eyes for a moment before looking back at me. His green eyes are filled with lust I want to quench. I lick my lips, ready and waiting as he grows closer, my entire body buzzing.

The door opens, and a cool breeze rushes between us.

"Shh... sweet girl, Mommy needs to sleep," Tre says, holding Ryah, who is crying loudly.

Guess the moment is over.

W e're told to return early from hitting the hills for a scavenger hunt. When I get back to our villa and find it empty, I decide to shower and get cleaned up. I was with Andrew, while Brynn went with Tre.

While I'm in the bathroom, I recall her touches from last night. The way Brynn's hand slid up the bottom of my sweatshirt and ran across my chest. My threadbare T-shirt doing nothing to keep the heat of her palm from searing into my skin.

I would never want to rush her, and when she told me she was ready to open the door to the possibility of something happening between us again the other night, it took every ounce of my willpower to remain cuddling on the couch rather than picking her up and taking her to bed.

Last night when Tre interrupted us, she withdrew quickly, and I missed her immediately.

We got up, and she folded the blanket and let Tre have the main house while we returned to our villa. But once we were inside, any hope that things would pick up where they left off were lost when she went into the bathroom and shut the door.

I was pretty sure she wasn't shaving and putting on a sexy outfit. More likely she was telling herself things were going too fast.

But that's okay. I'll wait for her. She's worth it.

I turn off the shower, sliding the glass door to the side and reaching for a towel when I hear her singing in the room beyond the door. The girl is Christmas all day every day, even down to the music she's listening to.

She's singing "All I Want For Christmas is You," and I smile, hoping like hell she's thinking of me.

I run the towel over my wet hair, eager to get dried off and join her. The bathroom door opens, and we both freeze.

She blinks and rushes out, slamming the door. "I'm so sorry, Pierce. I didn't hear you."

I wrap the towel around myself, step out of the shower, and open the door.

She's holding her AirPods in her palm. "I just saw the rental pull up and figured you were with Andrew, and I was lost in my music and..." Her gaze falls to my crotch.

"It's not like you haven't seen it before." I walk into the living area to grab some clothes.

"I know, but it's different now."

I chuckle and pick out some clothes. "It's not."

"Now I've seen it, and..."

I chuckle, stepping into my boxers then letting my towel fall. "I think you like what you saw."

She swallows, and her gaze slips again to my crotch. "Come on, what's not to like?"

"I appreciate the compliment."

She rolls her eyes. "I'm going to take a shower."

"I showed you mine, aren't you going to show me yours?" I grin at her.

She turns at the threshold to the bathroom. "Use your memory." She steps in and starts to shut the door.

146

"I need a refresher," I say, my eyes remaining on her.

Her hand falls from the door, and she steps out, grabbing the edge of her sweatshirt. Lord almighty, is she actually going to show me something?

Inch by inch, she lifts the fabric, then tears it off, revealing her thermals. At least the shirt is snug to her tits. I've never wanted my hands on something more than her.

I groan. "You're killing me."

She giggles. "Delayed gratification is a good thing." The door shuts.

"Not when it's this painful."

Laughter sounds from behind the door, and I hear the shower turn on.

I continue getting dressed, then plop down on the sofa. I really hope we get some more alone time soon.

* * *

We enter the main house and find Abe on a ladder, Gwen holding it to keep it steady. He's hanging something on the beam in front of the fireplace.

"What are you doing?" Brynn asks.

"We almost forgot the mistletoe. I found it in the bin with all the scavenger hunt supplies. Now if anyone gets caught under it, you have to kiss." Gwen waggles her eyebrows.

At least they waited until Brynn warmed up to me to hang it. It would have been painfully awkward to have her deny me in front of her entire family.

Abe steps down the ladder. "You know the tradition, honey—we're the first to kiss under it." He wraps his arm around Gwen and tugs her to his chest. She giggles until their lips meet, and they kiss. It's a conservative kiss, thank the lord.

Couple by couple, the rest join us, dressed and ready for the scavenger hunt, Nolan and Ryah in their strollers. Gwen and Abe hand out the sheets of paper that list what we need to find. There's nothing crazy on the list, and we should be able to find everything.

"Your mom and I aren't doing this one. First team back that has everything wins." Abe sits down. "Want to leave the kids?" He laughs since they're all bundled up.

"You could've told me before I wrestled with her to put a snowsuit on," Tre says, but unbuckles Ryah and hands her off to his dad.

Andrew does the same with Nolan. "This evens the odds."

"Oh god, are you going to make me run?" Kenzie asks, looking at Tessa as though maybe they should stay back too.

"We have to win at least one of these competitions." Andrew heads toward the door, but Kenzie pulls him back.

"Mistletoe," she says with a smile.

He stares longingly at the door but bends down and kisses Kenzie. When he gives her just a chaste kiss, she fists his jacket and keeps his lips where they are.

After what is an uncomfortable amount of time for all of us to witness, she releases him. "Remember at the end of this, you come to bed with me."

Andrew nods, and I laugh.

"I'm never getting married," Carter grumbles.

Faith huffs.

"It was a little hot," Carter continues. "She's got you by the balls though."

"My balls are very well intact. It's called compromise." Andrew faces Kenzie again. "And let me show you how you should really kiss your wife." He dips her and kisses her fully, making me turn away when I see tongue.

"Kids!" Brynn shouts.

"And this one is upset because she's not getting any." Carter thumbs in our direction.

"How about everyone just goes." Gwen waves, holding Nolan on her lap.

We all walk outside, and I'm determined to take charge of this one. I've sat back and allowed Brynn to spearhead the majority of the competitions, but I really want to win this for us and show off a little for her.

"Come on." I head toward the trail I saw the night I left her at the villa when I needed to be alone to center myself again. Thankfully, whatever Gwen said to her that night seemed to turn a new page for us. I'll always be grateful for that.

"Where are we going?" Brynn asks, and I slide my hand in hers.

"There's a trail I know where we can find everything." I look behind us and see that everyone has gone in their own directions.

"Just so you know, Tre was an army ranger, so we're probably not going to win this one," she says.

I stop us at the beginning of the trail. I'd forgotten about that. Still... "Where is my little competitive firecracker?"

She laughs. "Tired, and I'm not great at this part. I know my limitations and where my brothers excel."

I stare at her for a long beat, and she raises her eyebrows when I don't say anything right away. "You have no faith in me?"

"Well, you live in the city, and you don't seem very outdoorsy. You still use skis to get down the mountain."

I chuckle and shake my head. "What's with all the hate for skiers?"

"Nothing, but you're only thirty. Time to get on a board, buddy." She grins at me.

"Let me show you another side of me." I walk up the small hill and pick up a flat rock, dropping it in the bag Gwen gave us. "One down."

We continue up the path, and after I've found our fourth item, she finally starts getting into the search.

"Ew, moss, something soft." She picks it up, and I put it in the bag.

"See, isn't this fun?" I wrap my arm around her shoulders.

"I'll admit, I didn't think you were so observant, but you've found almost everything." She presses her lips to my neck. "Thank you."

Another hour goes by, and when we have everything, we walk down the trail toward the house, but I spot Tre and Tessa approaching from the other side.

"Ready to run?" I ask Brynn.

"Of course."

We increase our speed, trying not to let Tre and Tessa see us since they'll run too if they do.

"Damn it!"

I look back to see Brynn on the ground, face first in a mound of snow. She lifts her head, and it's red from the temperature of the ice.

"No way, victory is mine," Tre shouts and grabs Tessa's hand.

Brynn gets up but slips on the ice again. I bend down and pick her up, swinging her over my shoulder. No way am I letting Tre beat us. My eyes remain on Tre, narrowing as I clear the distance, jumping over a small bush.

"Jesus, I can run. Put me down," Brynn shouts.

Tre's practically dragging Tessa.

"Hello, I work at a bakery. I'm not running on a treadmill icing cupcakes. Slow down," Tessa barks at her husband, who looks just as determined as me.

We're all a few feet away from the door and increase our pace. I reach the door right before him, placing my hand on the doorknob, and Brynn almost slides off my shoulder.

"Damn it," Tre says.

I open the door and rush inside to find Gwen and Abe staring at us.

"Both people should have to walk in the door to be eligible for the win," Tre says.

"I could if someone would put me down," Brynn grumbles.

I lower Brynn's feet to the floor and drop our bag in front of Gwen and Abe.

"You guys were fast." Abe nods at both of us. "Impressive, Pierce. We figured this was Tre's win."

"It was, if you'd say that Brynn had to walk in on her own. He carried her the last quarter mile." Tre crosses his arms.

"My feet weren't exactly on the ground the whole time either." Tessa glares at her husband and picks up Ryah from Abe, who is sitting on the chair with her.

Tre blows out a breath.

"Looks like it's all here. You guys are the winners," Gwen says.

I grab Brynn and hug her. We do a little dance, then Abe clears his throat. We stop and look at him, and he glances above us.

Oh shit.

"Mistletoe for the winners," Tre says in a fake excited voice.

Tessa shakes her head but doesn't say anything.

Brynn's chest rises and falls as she meets my gaze. I glance at the small bunch of greenery with a red ribbon wrapped around it, then back down at Brynn. I give her a questioning look to ask permission, and she nods.

I lower my head, but the closer I get, the more I don't want to kiss her for the first time again here in front of her family. I want it to only be us, so I detour at the last second and kiss her cheek.

"Lame," Tre says. "They shouldn't win because they don't know how to kiss."

"Enough, Tre," Tessa says.

Whatever is in her tone makes me look closer at Brynn. I'm pretty sure it's disappointment that rests on her beautiful face.

The door opens and Andrew groans, bending over and heaving for breath. "Damn it."

"Well, that *wasn't* fun." Kenzie follows him in. "Carter and Faith are in their villa. They quit after about five minutes."

With all the commotion, I continue to stare at Brynn. She looks upset I didn't kiss her, but she just has to be patient. I have plans for us.

Chapter Twenty-Two

BRYNN

"Okay, I made some snacks, then we're going right into our next competition," my mom says.

"I'm tired," I say, feeling deflated that Pierce didn't kiss me on the lips under the mistletoe. Not to mention embarrassed.

I give him the green light, and he kisses my cheek. What the hell?

"I'm with Brynn," Kenzie says, yawning. "I love you all, but you're crazy."

"What's the next challenge?" Andrew asks.

"Oh, and next year we're not coming. You're turning my husband into you guys," Kenzie adds and yawns. "You must be injecting testosterone into the food or something."

"Stop being that way," Tessa says, sitting Ryah in her high chair and feeding her some of the snacks in bite-sized pieces.

"Well, we also have an early Christmas gift for you guys." Mom looks at Dad, who is walking in with a bunch of gift bags.

The only people here who don't know what the gifts are

would be Pierce and maybe Andrew and Kenzie. The rest of us groan.

"What?" Pierce asks me, eyes wary.

"You have to wait and see." I hop off the couch to grab something to eat.

I can't be upset with Pierce. I'm just upset in general. We've been toeing the line, and I'm a little butt-hurt that he didn't kiss me when he had the opportunity.

"Before we open them, we're going to have our snowman-making contest."

"Carter and Faith haven't returned from their afternoon delight." Tre pops a piece of caramel popcorn into his mouth. "Speaking of which, who wants to watch Ryah for an hour?"

"I will." I raise my hand.

Tessa shakes her head. "We're not going anywhere."

Tre blows out a breath.

"Then Carter and Faith will be disqualified. The rest of you can get going. We're not putting a time limit on this one. So go enjoy your day in the snow." Gwen points at the door.

"I feel like when we were kids, and they used to make us go outside when all we wanted to do was watch television," Tre says as we walk to the door like a herd of cattle.

Andrew places Nolan in his high chair, and my parents take over feeding the two of them.

"I like the built-in babysitter aspect of spending the holidays with your family, but I just want to go have a nice long nap now." Kenzie steps out into the sun, sits in one of the chairs, and rests her head back in her hands.

"You're the one with all the Christmas spirit," Andrew says, rolling some snow into a ball.

I sit next to Kenzie, while Tessa sits on my other side.

"I guess it's just us guys," Pierce says, way too excited to build a snowman.

The three of us watch them work, and eventually, I tilt my face up to the sun.

The guys decide that the best plan is to roll the snow into balls by starting behind the house and bringing them this way. Good luck to them.

Kenzie turns to face me. "So, you and Pierce, huh?"

"I've told him I want to give it a try."

Tessa sits up and looks at me. "Really?"

"Good for you." Kenzie places her gloved hand over mine.

"I thought you were looking cozy the other night. Tre said he walked in on something." Tessa grins.

"We almost kissed, but we haven't yet."

"Why?" Kenzie asks with a frown.

I shrug. "I wanted to take it slow, then once I was over that, Tre interrupted, and then we had the mistletoe…"

"And…?" Kenzie's forehead wrinkles.

"And he kissed her on the cheek," Tessa tells her for me.

Kenzie sucks in a breath.

"Yeah." My lips press together in a thin line.

Kenzie's about to say something, but all three of the men are pushing huge snowballs toward the front of the main house.

"Look, babe," Tre says to Tessa.

"Impressive," she says with a tone that suggests she's not actually impressed.

"What's in the gift bags from your parents?" Kenzie asks.

"Pajamas," Tessa, Tre, and I say in unison.

"And you're going to have to wear them." I bring my legs up to my chest and watch Pierce build the beginnings of a snowman.

I should probably go help him, so I lower my legs and scoot to the edge of my chair.

Kenzie grabs my jacket. "Don't you dare. If you help, we'll feel like we have to."

155

"You don't." I stand and go over to Pierce.

"You're mad," he whispers once I'm settled beside him.

I help him shape the snowman so that the second ball won't fall off the bottom one. "I'm not."

"Don't take the mistletoe thing to mean that I didn't want to kiss you," he says. "Because I do."

I smile. "Let's just finish this. I need a nap."

He lets the topic go, and we keep building the snowman. He's no frills for sure, but all of them are. Andrew is trying the hardest with the sticks he's gathered, turning one into a cane and trying to make a mustache from pine needles.

"Done," Pierce says.

"Great. I'm going to take a nap," I say and head toward the villa.

When I enter the code, I feel Pierce right behind me. "Me too. I need a refresh."

We walk in, and he groans at the couch, taking off his coat and boots.

"Sleep in the bed," I say.

"No, I'm fine." He picks up the blankets and pillows and puts them on the coffee table before taking the cushions off the couch.

"I'm serious. I'll sleep here."

He stares at the bed, and I feel guilty for hogging it this entire time.

"We can both sleep there," he says.

He's right, it's a king with plenty of room.

I strip down to my T-shirt and leggings and climb on the bed. And when the other side of the bed dips, I close my eyes.

"Can we spoon?" he asks.

I laugh. "You'll spoon me, but not kiss me?"

"Brynn." He sounds exasperated.

"I'm joking." I'm fully aware how passive-aggressive I'm

being. "But just so you know, whenever you want to kiss me, I'm okay with it."

"Good to know. Now sleep," he whispers, wrapping his arms around my middle from behind.

It isn't until I hear his steady breathing that I finally relax enough to fall asleep myself.

* * *

We all knew the gift was going to be pajamas, but we weren't prepared for us to have matching PJs with our partners.

I raise my eyebrows at Pierce, who is staring at the pajamas as though he doesn't understand how they work. They're the adult version of baby onesies, complete with feet and a zipper that runs from groin to sternum.

"You sleep in them," I say.

"I know that."

"You look confused." I take mine into the bathroom to change into them.

Since most of us napped or relaxed after the snowman competition, my parents delivered the pajamas to the benches outside our villas.

I come out of the bathroom to find Pierce putting on the pajamas, shaking his head.

"What?" I ask.

"I've done so much stuff out of my comfort zone this week."

"But we match!" I put out my arms in a *tada* pose.

He laughs and zips up. "I hope you're impressed."

I sit on the couch. "You didn't do it all for me. You're having fun."

"If you weren't here, I probably would have told Andrew I was sick and either stayed in my villa the entire time or gone home." He looks down at the ridiculous pajamas then sits down next to me.

"I had a really good nap," I admit.

"Me too." He smiles and bites his lip.

When is this man going to kiss me? I'll give him until tonight, but when we get back to this villa, I'm taking what I want with the hopes that he's on the same page as me. "We should go, otherwise we're going to be late."

"All right then."

We leave our villa in our coats and boots, spotting Carter and Faith coming out of their room at the same time. They're wearing matching green pajamas with reindeers on them.

"Don't you both look cute," I say.

"Same." Carter lifts his eyebrows at me.

"Nice of you to join us. As you can see, there are only three snowmen done." I wave at the yard. "It's not like you to pass up on not one, but two, challenges. What gives? You won last year, so you're ready to give up that spot on the tree to me?"

"It's not over yet," Carter challenges as I expected him to.

Maybe I'm wrong about the longevity of his and Faith's relationship, because he's spending a lot of time with her.

We all head inside, eat the meal Mom and Dad cooked for us, and finish up by watching *Miracle on 34th Street*. As expected, everyone heads to their villas as soon as the movie is done.

"I'll close up, Mom."

She smiles and takes her hand off the knob to turn off the gas fireplace. "Don't forget."

"We won't."

After my parents leave, I take the blanket off me and stand, yawning because I realize I'm ready for bed myself.

"I'm going to get a water, do you want one?" I ask Pierce,

heading into the kitchen. "Can you get the fireplace? Let's go back to the villa."

"Sure."

I grab two water bottles and head back toward the door. It takes me a moment to realize that Pierce is just standing by the fireplace, staring at me. My stomach whooshes when I realize he's standing under the mistletoe, and the fire is still going. He crooks his finger at me, and I walk toward him.

"What are you doing?" I ask quietly.

He takes the bottles out of my hands and places them on the coffee table.

"Pierce, you don't have to." I hope I didn't pressure him into this.

"I'm doing what I wanted to earlier, but..." He steps closer to me, his hand cradling my cheek. "I wasn't going to kiss you again for the first time in front of your family. I wanted it to be a moment shared between just the two of us. One we'd both remember."

"Oh," I say, feeling foolish for being upset.

"And I wanted it like this, right here. Me and you, a roaring fireplace, and us under the mistletoe."

"Yeah?"

He chuckles. "Yeah. Can I kiss you now, Brynn?"

"You better."

He lowers his head, and his lips meet mine. Familiarity and desire bloom in my chest. The six years of separation disappear, and there's a natural ease between us that isn't found when you kiss a stranger.

A low current moves through the warmth and tenderness of his lips. His tongue slides into my mouth, and it's a rekindling of our passion. All the memories from that weekend flood back into my mind, and I push away the regret that's accompanied them for too long. He's right here, and we're together again, so I rise on my tiptoes, running my fingers up and over his shoulders, offering myself to him.

His hands wind around my waist, tugging me toward him so that our bodies are flush. He deepens the kiss, his tongue sliding along mine. But when he slows the kiss, his lips moving off mine, I whimper because I wasn't ready yet.

Pierce trails his mouth down my jaw. "I never forgot how you tasted," he whispers. "And I can't wait to taste every inch of you again."

My core heats, and I clench my thighs, needing a lot more than kissing to satisfy what's blossoming inside me. In my head, I told myself I'd take it slow, but I want him. I want him naked and on top of me. I want him in my mouth, and I want his mouth on me.

"Take me back to our villa," I say.

"My pleasure." He slides his hand into mine, turns off the fireplace, and we lock up the lodge before walking back to our villa.

Pierce presses the code, and opens the door, turning on the light.

"Oh shit." He slams the door shut.

"What?"

"Um..." He turns around. "Stay here."

I pull him back by his jacket. "What is it?"

"I think I saw a rat or something scurry by when I opened the door."

There goes me getting laid tonight.

Chapter Twenty-Three

PIERCE

I'm not big on rodents, but I'm also not willing to look like a wimp in front of Brynn.

"I'll be back," I say, opening the door a second time, determined to catch this critter so I can finally have Brynn under me again.

"I'll go with you," she says, her hands clinging to the back of my pajamas.

"You don't have to."

"I don't want to be out here by myself. I'm sure the little guy has friends."

We tiptoe into the villa, and she slams the door.

"You're going to scare him."

The critter runs from under the couch to under the bed.

Brynn screeches and jumps around me onto the couch cushions. "I can't."

"Which is why I told you to wait outside," I say, heading toward the bed.

"And I told you he has friends out there. It could be an entire plan. He's the decoy."

I chuckle and look at her for a second. "New thing I learned about you—you have an active imagination."

"You have no idea if what I'm saying is false."

I pick up a shoe by Brynn's suitcase and toss it under the bed to hopefully get the rodent out.

"Use your own shoe!" she shouts.

"Our bigger problem is that there's nothing in this villa for me to trap him with, so we're going to have to resort to scaring him enough that he runs out the door." I raise my eyebrows in question because this means she has to help.

"You want me to open the door, don't you?" She bites her lip.

"Would you prefer to be the one who scares it?"

"I'd rather not do either."

"Sorry, that's not an option." I'm standing next to the bed when the little thing runs out from under the bed at full speed toward the bathroom.

I jump up on the bed. "Bloody hell, he's fast."

"Pierce." Her body squirms, and she wretches as if she's going to throw up.

"Okay. Okay." I step down from the bed, peeking into the bathroom. "I was wrong, it's not a rat."

"What is it then?" Her eyes are wide and filled with fear.

"A mouse."

She groans. "Not much better."

"I find it a little more comforting." I shake out my body and look back at her. "Okay, get ready. Full disclosure, I have no idea what I'm doing here."

"What?" she practically screeches.

I jump in front of the door to scare the mouse. It runs out of the bathroom. Brynn screams and scares it back my way, but I try to block its path.

"Open the door," I shout.

She screams, hopping off the couch and running on her

tiptoes to the door. "Please no friends. Please no friends." She closes her eyes in blind faith.

I chase the critter, and I don't react when he circles around Brynn. Good thing her eyes are closed because she doesn't want to see this. Having nowhere to go and giving up his new home, he scurries out of the villa. I take the door from Brynn, slamming it.

"Is he gone?" she says, her eyes still closed tightly.

"He is."

Her head falls back, and I expect her to feel relieved, but she runs by me and back onto the couch. "We should do a full sweep."

"He left," I say, walking over to her.

"Maybe he came in here with a friend?" Her voice is pleading.

I groan. I don't want to go on a search for another mouse. I want to sit on this couch and make out with her. "You said his friends were outside."

She shrugs. "We don't know how mice think."

"Clearly they're geniuses according to you." I take out my phone and put on my flashlight.

"Look under the furniture too," she says.

So I do, because I'll do about anything to get this over with and get back to her being my sole attention.

"The bed!" she shouts. "Don't forget the bed!"

I turn back around, and she shrugs.

"Sorry, just want to make sure. You're doing great." She raises her fist in the air like "go team."

I check the rest of the villa, thankful it's small. When I come back to the couch, Brynn finally sits, bringing her knees up to her chest.

"No friends." I sit next to her.

"Good. Thank you."

I slide my hand under her bent knees and pull them to rest over my lap.

The mood from under the mistletoe has been destroyed by a small rodent.

Thanks a lot, mouse.

I place my hands on her foot and massage it.

Her head rocks back, and she stretches. "That feels good."

"I'm glad."

We sit in silence except for her moans that make my dick stir. I'd love to take her to bed tonight. My hands slide up her legs, massaging her calf, and I start to think I can turn this night back around.

Until something crashes in the bathroom.

She bolts up, her head almost hitting mine. "What was that?"

It turns out to be the shampoo in the shower, but it doesn't matter. It's not happening tonight.

Chapter Twenty-Four

BRYNN

Thankfully, Pierce didn't try anything last night. There was no way I was going to be relaxed enough after the mouse episode, and the next time we have sex, I don't want to be lost in my head thinking some rodent is peering over his shoulder as Pierce thrusts into me.

It's our second-to-last competition, and Pierce and I are tied with Tre and Tessa. Andrew and Kenzie finally got on the board with the snowman competition. Carter has obviously given up, and my parents are disqualified because of tapping out on too many events. It's harder for everyone to participate with Ryah and Nolan here, but none of us would change it for the world.

"We're swapping," Dad says.

"Okay, this contest thing has gone too far," Carter says.

"What are you talking about?" Tre phrases the question better, although I think I speak for all of us Russell siblings that hearing the word swapping out of my dad's mouth gave us all the ick.

"Get your mind out of the gutter." Dad smacks the back

of Carter's head. "If you usually use skis, you're riding a snowboard today and vice versa. First one down the hill wins this competition." Dad smiles at all of us.

Pierce leans in closer to my ear and whispers, "I've never snowboarded before."

"I guess that changes today."

"Bloody hell." He shakes his head.

Tre glances at me and gives me a smug smile because he and Tessa are both snowboarders. Everyone knows it's easier to move to skis than to snowboards.

"We have to come first to ensure we have a chance at winning the whole thing," I say. "The last event is the one Carter thought of, and my assumption is he'll actually try to win that one since it's his. And do we really want to try to melt an ice sculpture without using anything but our hands and mouth?"

Pierce shakes his head, but he looks really afraid.

This isn't looking good for us.

"Good thing you have me to help this time around." I infuse my voice with false confidence.

"No more talking about tactics. Get your stuff and get on those lifts. Your mom and I will be at the bottom of the hill with the kids." Dad points at the door. "See you in a bit."

We swap out the equipment we can from one person to the next and rent the stuff we can't. An hour later, we're all waiting to get on the lift while Mom and Dad wave at us, getting Ryah and Nolan to do the same.

"So, keep your weight centered over your board, bend your knees, try not to catch your edge when you do your turns, and don't go straight down."

Pierce shakes his head. "How upset will you be if we lose?" I stare blankly at him, and he nods. "A lot. Okay. No pressure." He blows out a breath.

"Of course I'm not going to be upset."

I'll be bummed, but I'm not so competitive that I'd be mad about a loss. It's more about the fact that I want to win, and I feel disappointed if I don't.

"Somehow I don't believe you," he says.

The lift comes to an end, and we get off with Tre and Tessa right behind us, skiing like fucking pros.

"We're going to look so good at the top of the tree," Tre says, passing us while I ski slowly next to Pierce, who is holding his snowboard under his arm.

We all get to the top of the hill. At least Andrew looks just as freaked out as his cousin. Kenzie glances at me and cringes. It is a little scary that someone, meaning Andrew or Pierce, might end up in the emergency room if this goes badly.

"Okay, let's get you strapped in." I help Pierce get his feet in and lock them in place. "Remember what I said."

He nods. I put my goggles in place and look down the row. Carter and Faith might be a contender too. She's really athletic, and they're on skis just like Tre and Tessa.

Clearly, the disadvantaged ones are us and Kenzie and Andrew.

We all stare at one another, start the countdown, and push off to start our descent.

Andrew falls immediately.

Pierce holds his own for a little longer but ends up on his ass, cringing in pain.

Tessa loses a ski farther down, and Faith is doing the pizza stance slow as a turtle. This is good for us.

I help Pierce back up. He's athletic, so he gets it for a little bit, but getting down this mountain is no quick feat.

Tre helps Tessa, and they start back down the hill.

The leading team changes back and forth most of the way, but when I can see the bottom, I'm proud of Pierce for sticking to it, since I'm pretty sure I heard Andrew tell Kenzie that he was done five falls ago. I fully expect him to be walking down the mountain.

Faith got off track, and Carter had to set her straight, so we're in front of them.

I'm sure Tre and Tessa are already done and waiting at the bottom with their winning smiles.

"Tre fell." Pierce points to his right.

I look past him, lifting my goggles. Sure enough, both of Tre's skis are off, and Tessa is getting out of hers to help him. This is our chance.

"I feel like I shouldn't have told you that. You have that look in your eyes," Pierce says.

"It's fine, but we have a chance now. You're going longer every time before you fall. You got this!" I put my goggles back on and slide behind him, prepared to guide him down.

"What are you doing?" he asks.

"Ensuring our win." I sneak a peek at Tre and Tessa. He's about to get into his skis.

I push Pierce with my hand on his hip and my skis on either side of his board.

"Whoa!" Pierce says when he wobbles from the speed.

"Remember, knees bent and center your gravity," I say.

"You said not to go straight. I don't feel like I'm in control." Pierce glances over his shoulder at me.

"Eyes forward." My hands are on his hips, and my attention wavers back to Tre.

He's up on his skis, pushing off with the poles. Tessa is right behind him.

I know I can get us to that finish line before them.

"This is fast," Pierce says, but I'm too busy making sure we reach the bottom first.

Our momentum builds, and I'm having a hard time

keeping my hands on his hips. Soon, I grasp for Pierce's jacket, but he's inches, then an entire foot in front of me.

"Brynn!" he shouts.

I cringe, but he's moving so fast I can't catch him. When someone gets in his way, he manages to pivot away. Oh, I'm kind of proud.

I push off with the poles and race down to meet him, seeing that Tre and Tessa aren't close enough behind us to win.

Pierce's yell pulls my attention back to him—right before he barrels into the orange fencing, slipping over it.

Shit.

I ski down to him. "Oh my god! Are you okay?"

He sits on the board still attached to his feet while blood trickles down his forehead.

"Crap, you're bleeding."

"Way to put your boyfriend in the hospital to win," Tre says, patting me on the back.

"You're just a sore loser." I look back at Pierce. "Not that I'm okay with you getting hurt."

He nods. Maybe I need to look into this competitive fire inside me.

"Hate to see what happens if he gets the job over you," Tre says and skis off with Tessa.

Tre's always been a sore loser, so I don't care.

I crouch next to Pierce. "I'm sorry."

He smiles. "It's okay. We won, didn't we? A little cut isn't too bad."

He really is great.

"I promise to kiss your boo boo," I whisper.

"Then let's get the hell out of here." He unstraps his feet from the board, and I unclip my boots from the skis.

Now we just have to make sure Tessa and Tre don't win at

the ice sculpture melting contest to make it a tie. If so, it'll be mine and Pierce's picture on the top of the tree next year.

But I can't help the gnawing feeling in my gut about what Tre said. We haven't really addressed the Mancini Advertising job. How will we navigate it if one of us gets it over the other?

Problems for another day, I suppose.

Chapter Twenty-Five

PIERCE

I knew Brynn was competitive, but as we ride back to the villas with tissues pressed against my bloody head, I realize I didn't know to what extent.

At the same time, it was thrilling to win. The thought that maybe I'll be around next year to have my picture on top of the tree is as welcome as it is terrifying.

I actually might try out snowboarding again. With her help and instruction, I felt as though I could get to a point where I could really get the hang of it.

"She just pushed you, dude," Carter says from the front seat.

"Shut up, Carter," Brynn says. She's been kind of quiet on the ride and keeps looking at me as though she feels bad.

"I don't know why you'd do that to him Brynn," Tre says from the driver's seat.

I'm not sure how we got into Tre's SUV, but it was a scramble after my fall. Plus, Tre was a medic in the army. I thought for sure it would be Gwen checking me out.

"It's because of you two that I'm so competitive." Brynn crosses her arms.

Carter and Tre look at one another and laugh.

"You're blaming us?" Carter points at his chest as though he can't imagine what she's saying to be true.

"You always excluded me! If I wanted to catch up and hang out with you, I had to be as good as you at something. Beat you."

"I don't remember a lot of wins, Brynn." Carter looks at Tre.

Brynn's eyes narrow. "Maybe because I'm half your size and years younger."

Hearing her animosity, I understand now why she's so competitive when it comes to this Christmas contest.

"Still... you pushed him." Tre looks at me through the rearview mirror.

"I'm fine," I repeat for what feels like the thousandth time.

"Not to mention, you didn't win yet. There's still the last competition. Tessa and I can tie you, then it'll go to a tie-breaker."

"Bring it on. I know how to use my hands." Brynn huffs and crosses her arms again.

"Ew." Carter's head whips in my direction, giving me a scathing look. "I don't want to think about you giving Pierce a hand job."

"That's not what I meant, and please, you've been all over Faith the entire trip. You guys barely leave your villa."

Carter shrugs with a cocky smirk. "She can't get enough of me."

"All right, let's just be quiet the rest of the ride," Tre says.

"Since when did you turn into Dad?" Brynn says with an eye roll.

"Yeah, quit being so fucking bossy," Carter adds.

Tre grunts and keeps his eyes on the road.

I'm thankful when we reach the area our villa is in. I need a little break from the Russell sibling back and forth.

"Christmas is almost here, then you can go back to New York and not worry about me being bossy." Tre blows out a breath.

"Ah... I'm just kidding. You know I miss you." Carter lays his head on his brother's shoulder.

Tre pushes it off, and Carter laughs.

"And now both you assholes are gonna be in New York," Tre says.

I glance at Brynn as her smile dips.

"Ryah won't have any aunts or uncles in Portland," Tre says, and I catch him and Brynn making eye contact through the mirror.

"I'll FaceTime all the time. And come home a lot. But as of right now, we don't even know if I got the job, nor if I would even take it."

My head whips to the side. "Why wouldn't you take it?"

Neither Tre nor Carter comment. I think they're waiting to hear Brynn's answer too.

She shrugs. "I don't know. I'm trying not to think about it. It's a big decision."

I understand what she means. I'd be moving from an entirely different country to take the job. The only thing I'm abundantly clear about is that I want out of teaching and to see if I can hack it in the real world.

"True." I look out the window at the snowflakes falling onto the wet pavement. My future is so up in the air, I can't help but wonder where I'll land.

Tre parks outside the villas, and I open the door to climb out.

"Need me to hold you up? Hate for you to pass out from blood loss." Carter tries to put his hand on my arm.

"I'm good, mate."

Brynn walks with me to our villa, presses the code, and opens the door, allowing me to go in first.

PIPER RAYNE

"Have a seat on the couch. I'm going to grab the first aid kit I saw under the bathroom sink." She takes off her coat and her boots while I do the same.

I sit on the couch, and she disappears into the bathroom.

This couldn't be more embarrassing. I reprimand my younger self for not trying to master snowboarding earlier in life.

"Okay." She straddles my knees, sliding to the edge of the coffee table, and opens the small red bag. "I'm going to clean it first."

I watch her open the small foil packet and pull out what I know is going to sting my skin.

"Want something to hold?" she asks.

"I'm not five years old, Brynn, just do it."

She stares at me.

"Sorry, bruised ego," I grumble.

She giggles. "No reason for that. My brothers are right, I took it a little far. I should be the one to apologize."

"I'll forgive you if you come up here and straddle my lap." I lean forward and run my hands up her thighs.

"Well…" She stands and flutters her eyelashes. "If I must."

Resting one knee on one side of my outer thigh and the other one next to my other one, she sits her arse on my thighs. I put my hands on her hips, running them up and down her ribcage.

"Am I forgiven now?" she asks.

I slide my hands down to her ass and pull her closer, so she can feel my dick perking up to attention. "Now you are."

"Lucky me."

Her tits look fucking amazing in her tight thermal shirt. I'm really hoping I get to see what's under it today.

My hands fidget with the hem of her shirt, my fingers slipping under the thin fabric. "Is this okay?"

"Playing with your nurse's breasts while she's trying to

174

take care of your wound is dangerous." She lifts that alcohol wipe.

"Maybe I do need to hold on to something." I glide my knuckles up her ribs, the shirt rising with my movements.

"I do like to make sure my patients are comfortable." Her breath hitches as I reach the cups of her bra.

Her pebbled nipples poke out from the silk fabric, and my dick is up between our bodies. She raises her arms, and I lift her shirt off her body. God, she's so gorgeous. Her skin looks soft and silky and inviting.

"Ready?" she asks.

"In a minute." I tug down the cups of her bra, resting the fabric under the weight of her tits, then I run my thumbs across her nipples, and she inhales a deep breath.

"Pierce." She says my name as if I'm her savior.

I so want to give her everything we've both been wanting for too long. "I thought you were going to clean me up."

She quirks an eyebrow.

"My cute, dirty girl."

She lifts the swab, and I tug her forward, my mouth covering her nipple right as the alcohol stings my cut.

"Hell..." She continues to pat it, and I moan around her nipple in part from pain and part from pleasure.

When I twirl her nipple with my tongue, she drops the swab, and it falls to the coffee table.

"You're making this very difficult, Mr. Wainwright." She bends over to get a Band-Aid.

"I'm sorry, are my clothes in the way?" I say, moving my mouth to her other tit, giving her other nipple equal attention.

"They are a little cumbersome, but we're almost done. I don't think you need stitches. We'll cover it with a Band-Aid and see how it holds up, but I'd refrain from physical exertion for a few hours." She places the Band-Aid over my cut and tosses the wrapping next to the alcohol pad.

"I'm sorry, nurse, that's just not going to be possible." My finger dips into the elastic waistband of her pants.

"Why not?" she asks in a breathy voice.

"Because I have this girl I slept with six years ago, and I just got another chance with her. Wound be damned, nothing is going to stop me from giving her what she wants."

"And what do you think she wants?" She rises onto her knees, giving me access to slide my palm down her pants, past the barrier of her underwear.

I run a finger through her wetness. "I think she wants my cock."

She laughs, but it dies quickly when I slowly circle my thumb over her clit.

"Maybe my hand is enough actually," I whisper, placing a kiss on her collarbone.

"It's not."

"Good." My mouth moves to her tits once again as I push one, then two fingers into her.

She's wet and ready and loves me sucking on her tits. They're more than a handful and the perfect size for her frame. She says my name again in that throaty voice laced with desire.

"Just enjoy." I use my thumb to rub her clit while I finger her.

She bears down on my hand, her fingers digging into my shoulders as her breathing increases. The little sounds falling from her mouth tell me she's almost there, and I'm desperate to see her fall apart. Her body rocks back, and I plunge two fingers inside her while my thumb still circles her clit. I increase my pace, and her forehead drops to mine.

Her breath floats over my face. "Shit. It feels so good. Don't stop."

"Wouldn't dream of it."

She rocks into my palm back and forth until she sucks in a

breath and lets it out in a rush, her orgasm running through her body. Exquisite. I could watch her like this all bloody day.

Her hands go to my pants, tugging and pulling at them. I raise my hips off the couch, and she stands to help slide them down my legs, along with my boxer briefs. Next goes my shirt.

Then Brynn pulls down her pants and panties, almost falling over on the couch trying to get them off her feet. I steady her hips, and she drops back into my lap, removing her bra. "You have a condom, right?"

"In my bag," I say, nodding toward my computer bag on the floor. I go to scoot her off, but she splays her hand on my chest.

"I've got it."

I watch her naked body bend down, and my dick twitches. "Front pocket," I instruct to get us there faster.

She opens the zipper and sticks her hand in, moving it all around. "You have a lot of stuff in here," she says, pulling out some receipts, my ChapStick, my keys... Her body freezes over top of mine. Her legs slide off my thighs, and she sits on her ankles on the other cushion, holding up my keys. Specifically, the keychain I bought for her six years ago. "Pierce?"

This might actually be more embarrassing than falling down a mountain.

Chapter Twenty-Six

BRYNN

It can't be the same keychain, but it looks identical.

"Do we have to have this conversation while we're naked?" he asks, cringing.

"Why do you have this?"

He sighs and meets my gaze. "I was never able to give it to you. We forgot it when you left that Sunday, and I was going to give it to you on Monday at dinner, but..."

He doesn't need to finish. We both know how that played out.

"I know all that. Not the Monday thing, but why is it on your keys?"

He runs a hand down his face before wrapping it around that back of his neck, tugging. "Do I have to answer?"

I smile at him, my chest warming. "I'd like an answer."

"Hell, Brynn." He blows out a breath. "Because it reminded me of you. Of that weekend we spent together."

"Aw..." I straddle his waist again, feeling his hardening length against my core. "That's so sweet." I place a soft kiss on his lips.

"You don't find it creepy?" He rocks his head back into the cushion. The red tint of his cheeks tells me how uncomfortable and embarrassed he is.

I sprinkle kisses along his jaw, trailing down his neck. "Not at all."

"I was going to give it to you on the last day of the semester, but you didn't show."

I press my lips down the hollow of his neck, licking over his Adam's apple. "I had to go home early because my grandpa was having surgery."

"I heard afterward. Professor Jorgensen told me. So, I put it on my keys that day and just never took it off."

My hands roam down the front of his chest and back up the sides as I nuzzle as close to him as I can get. "You missed me."

His hand wraps around my neck, pulling my lips off his body. "Without question. I missed you every fucking day."

I can't fight the smile on my face because as hard as I tried to rip him from my memories, he always came floating back, never giving me the choice but to long for what we experienced in our short time together.

"Hey, Pierce." I lift the condom in front of his face. "How about you show me how much you missed me?"

His hands go to my ass, and he stands, lifting me at the same time. He carries me to the bed and lays me down, crawling over me. I relish the weight of him sinking me into the plush mattress.

He captures my mouth, sliding his tongue through my parted lips. I lose myself in his kiss, in his exploration of my body. His hard length presses against my hip, and I inch my knee to the side, letting his hips find their way between my thighs. His tip presses against my opening.

"I need you." I shift my hips side to side.

But he doesn't say anything, his lips continuing to make invisible pathways along my skin.

Over the years, I forgot the way he lets me lose myself. All my problems, concerns, worries, and insecurities vanish when I'm with him. It's so freeing, I could become addicted. Who am I kidding? I'm already addicted to him.

"I know, but I've waited years to feel you again, and I don't want to rush this."

Fair enough.

He wiggles down my body, situating himself between my legs. His warm hands slide up my inner thighs, widening them further to fit his shoulders.

"This good?" he asks, and I nod, unable to hide the tremble working through my body. A shiver runs up my spine from seeing him mere inches from my mound, the smirk on his face as if he's been waiting his entire life. "I remember how much you liked it last time."

I laugh. "You do not."

"Are you testing my memory?" he asks, his cocky smirk turning into a wicked grin. "If I remember correctly, you liked it when I blew on it." He purses his lips and blows a hot breath.

Another shiver races up my spine. I moan, my hand slipping down to thread through his hair.

"And you liked it when I did this." He nibbles the inside of each of my thighs, licking the spot right after to ease the sting.

My back sinks further into the mattress as I arch my hips.

"And you loved my teasing." He places gentle kisses closer and closer to my center, his large palms wrapping around my legs.

I swallow the saliva filling my mouth.

"Then your eyes rolled back when I took a deep inhale of you." His nose nudges along my clit, and I hear his intake of breath.

Holy hell, he's taking me to the brink, and he's barely touched me.

"Most of all, you loved it when my face was buried." He grips my ass, tugging me forward. "My tongue. Remember my tongue?" He drags the tip of his tongue from my clit down to my opening and back up again.

My free hand grips the comforter, and I arch my hips again.

"You smell just as good as I remembered." He sucks my clit, his tongue lazily circling, and I become dizzy from the pleasure he's giving me.

My legs become weightless as he laps me up.

"Pierce," I moan.

He strips his mouth off me, and I whimper. Rising up to my elbows, I stare down the length of my body at his face between my thighs.

"Like what you see?" he asks.

"Very much."

He chuckles and buries his face back in my pussy, but this time he increases his speed, taking me to the edge so fast, I want to repeat the process. I grip his hair, and he groans, feasting on me, his tongue teasing my opening, his nose running along my sensitive clit. When I can't take any more, his hands slide up my body, reaching for my tits and pinching my nipples.

My ass rises off the mattress, bucking, needing the friction, desperation clawing at my insides. And then it comes, barreling down on me, and I'm unable to stop it before I'm crying out, trying to close my thighs from it all feeling like too much.

He slows down, and the stars that fill my eyes finally clear.

Rising on my elbows, I watch as he pushes up and sits back on his ankles, wiping his face with the back of his hand. My insides clench.

"As good as you remembered?" He rips open the wrapper and slides the condom down his thick length before chuckling and falling over me.

"Cocky, huh?"

He sears my lips with his, and I wrap my arms around his neck, losing myself in him again.

"Want to ride me? I'm gonna feign not remembering."

I push on his chest, and he flips to his back. Straddling him, I hold the base of his cock and sink down on him.

"Bloody hell," he says when he's fully seated inside me.

"Yeah." I rock back and forth slowly at first, his hands on my hips.

The way his fingernails press into my flesh, I realize he's far from needing anything slow. So I ride him faster, my hands on his chest, the light sprinkling of his chest hair running through my splayed palms. He looks magnificent below me, and I realize quickly that I could get used to this life.

"You feel so damn good." His voice is a rough whisper.

"So do you."

I'm not always a three-orgasm girl, but I feel the tingle at the base of my spine. He palms my breasts, tweaking my nipples, and I arch my back, placing my hands on his thighs, rocking along his length.

"You look so good riding my dick," he says, causing my orgasm to gain another notch. "Your pussy is so tight."

It's the struggle in his voice, the one that says he's barely holding on that makes me feel powerful. I'm the one able to bring him to this point, just like he did me when his face was between my thighs.

He flips me, picking up one leg and resting it on his shoulder, and when he thrusts into me, he's so deep, I cry out. "Oh. My. God."

"Jesus, Brynn."

183

He hammers into me, and I can hear how wet I am with every plunge.

"I can't..." I clench down, not wanting to come yet, and he growls.

I grip his flexed forearms, the corded muscles bulging, and tighten my hold, reaching a height of pleasure I can no longer contain. My muscles tense, and I stop breathing as my climax overtakes me.

"Brynn, you're killing me," he pants.

A warm feeling as though I'm the gooey center of a lava cake floods me, and I look up at Pierce. Sweat beads on his forehead, and his eyes are overflowing with lust.

He sinks into me and withdraws only halfway before sinking in again. Over and over until he comes on a curse and a moan.

He collapses on me, but quickly rises onto his elbows and pushes the hair away from my eyes. "You good?"

I giggle because three orgasms later? Yeah, I'm good. "I'm great. You?"

He grins at me. "Same. I'll be right back." Pierce slips out of me.

I hear him in the bathroom, and when he returns, he pulls back the sheets and slides under them, waiting for me to join him.

"Thank you," he says after our breathing calms, and our sweat has dried.

"For what?" I look up at him.

"Giving me another chance." His finger runs along my hairline, moving my crazy hair out of the way again as if he needs to be staring into both of my eyes. "I was always so worried about making a life for myself after being at the mercy of so many others growing up that I sacrificed you, and I never should have."

I kiss his chest. "Maybe this was just our path. Maybe that wasn't our time six years ago."

He nods. "It's our time now though."

I smile. "I think so too."

I lay my head on his chest, and we decide to skip family movie night and enjoy one another over and over.

Chapter Twenty-Seven

PIERCE

At breakfast the next morning, the Russells all give us the look. The look that says they know why we skipped the movie last night.

"To be really nice, we watched *Die Hard* last night." Carter pats Brynn on top of her head.

She moves out of his way, and I slide her a cup of coffee.

"We're not sure where all the screams were coming from though." Carter fist-bumps Tre on the way to the table.

"You guys are all so funny." Brynn shoots me an apologetic look, but I shake my head.

Tessa walks in, freshly showered and appearing as though she's ready to go somewhere. She spots Brynn at the counter. "Hey, remember I was telling you about that marketing rundown for the bakery business?"

"Yeah."

"Well, I talked to Ava this morning, and she wants to go through with it. Can you get something together when we get back?"

Tre comes over and kisses his wife. "You look beautiful."

"It's what happens when you get to sleep in and take more than a minute shower. Thank you." She kisses him back.

Brynn pushes Tre. "Take your mushy stuff somewhere else."

"I figured you'd be more accommodating since you'll be doing mushy stuff too now." Tre sticks out his tongue and takes his coffee to the table, releasing a huge yawn.

"So?" Tessa asks, turning the conversation back to the marketing for her bakery.

"Yeah. For sure. And we have Pierce too. I'm sure he can help."

Tessa looks at me. "Okay. Perfect." She slides off the stool. "Kenzie and I are going shopping. Are you sure you don't mind babysitting, Gwen? We can bring the kids with us."

"And get nothing accomplished? Go have a girls' day." Gwen waves them off.

"Do you want to go?" I whisper to Brynn, not wanting her to turn down an invitation just to spend time with me.

"I politely declined their invitation because I'd rather shop with you."

"Me too." I walk around the counter and kiss her temple.

"K.I.S.S.I.N.G—"

"Carter, stop," Abe says.

Carter acts exasperated that he's being told no. "This is too good not to make jokes."

"You're not twelve," Abe says.

Gwen and I put out the food, and everyone sits around the table, eating breakfast.

Afterward, Brynn and I go back to the villa, shower, and get ready to go shopping. We call an Uber, so the rental SUV is available for everyone else. The guys are going to the ski hill, and Gwen and Abe need a car just in case something happens.

I link my hand with Brynn's in the back of the Uber. She

smiles at me, and the feeling of having her with me like this again settles into my chest.

We're dropped off downtown near the small shops, and the entire street is decorated in a holiday theme. It's festive, and this is the first time since I was young that the red, white, and green decor makes me cheerful. I was always so indifferent to it after my parents passed away.

As an adult, I'd go to my aunt and uncle's or some other distant relative's house for Christmas dinner, where most would ask about my job, if I had a girl, and other superficial level questions.

It's different with the Russells. They know each other so well. So much so that it's scary at times. They're all so invested in each other's lives and happiness and well-being. Sure, Andrew clearly cares about me, but this is next level.

"It's so pretty, right? Want to snap a picture together?" Brynn pulls out her phone.

"Sure."

"Good, I have to show off the man in my life." She leans into my chest.

I grab the phone from her hand, snapping the picture of the two of us with a winter wonderland in the background. She really amazes me. After giving me the cold shoulder and pushing me away, as soon as she decided to give me a chance, she's all in. Her blind trust is inspiring.

"So, what are we shopping for?" she asks as I place my hand in hers to lead us down the walkway.

"I have to get your family some gifts. I didn't have a chance to shop in New York. I went from the interview right to Andrew and Kenzie's."

"You don't have to get my family anything."

"I do. You can help me pick out some things."

"Spending other people's money? Sign me up." She laughs and drags me into the first store we come across.

We end up browsing through the place. I pick up a snow globe and shake it around before setting it down.

"Don't you love those?" Brynn picks one up and shakes it, watching the snow whirl around the slopes of Utah in the glass dome. Her smile reminds me of myself so many years ago.

It feels as if there's a pit in my stomach.

"They're okay," I say, moving on to look at funny signs about skiers versus snowboarders.

"Hey…" She comes over to me, linking her arm through mine. "I feel like I'm missing something here."

I shrug, not wanting to ruin our day by dumping another shit story at her feet. "It's nothing. You should get one if you love them. Actually, let me." I start to walk over to the snow globes, but she doesn't budge.

"Pierce?"

I blow out a breath and stare at the table filled with what I thought at one point were magic globes. I turn back around to face her.

"It's nothing." I shake my head, but she tilts her head, clearly waiting for me to say more. "Want to walk for a minute?"

She nods. We leave the store, and once we're a ways away from it, I turn to her.

"My mum loved snow globes and used to put them out at Christmas. We would shake them all really fast, making a game of it, and pick the one where we thought the snow would fall the fastest. If I picked right, I got a Christmas cookie."

How can the memories of her and my dad still pierce my heart like the day I found out they died? People told me that over time my memories would turn happy, but for me, that hasn't happened. I'm still bitter that they were taken from me.

"That's so sweet." She lifts on the balls of her feet and kisses me. Her nose is chilled from the weather. "What happened to them?"

Here comes the bad part, so I look at her, wanting to warn her that this will hurt. "I was allowed to keep one after they died. I picked this one my mum and I bought the Christmas before they died. It was supposed to be the North Pole. That was the year I stopped believing and told her as much. She picked it out and said that if Santa wasn't real, then how were people able to design a globe with the North Pole inside like they did for all the other cities in the world. I played her game because I didn't want to hurt her feelings, and it seemed really important to her that I believe still.

"I used to lie in my bed at boarding school and shake it, and her words would repeat in my head. It would take me back to that moment, and I would feel her with me."

She wraps her arms around my middle, and I kiss the top of her head. I feel as if I'm back in therapy, but I don't want anything to come between us. In this relationship, I'm the one carrying all the baggage.

"Do you still have it?" she whispers.

"No." My voice is hoarse.

"Why not?"

I swallow the lump in my throat. "Well, Tommy McDonald."

She draws back. "Do I need to kick his ass?"

I chuckle. "No. He was a bully and an asshole and is probably in debt now after spending all his trust fund."

"What did he do?"

I tighten my arms around her. "Smashed it."

She gasps. "Why?"

"Because he knew it was important to me."

"Yeah, but why did he bully you?"

"Because I didn't fight back. Because I was quiet and reserved. He said all I did was stare at it all day."

She sighs. "You were a boy who'd lost his parents."

I shake my head. "To him, I was just the boy who wasn't

fawning over him and making him believe he was a big deal. He thought I was weak..."

"And?" This woman catches everything.

"I'm not proud of how I reacted."

"Okay..." She waits for me to continue.

"After he broke it, I tackled him to the ground, jumped on top of him, and hit him over and over. I didn't stop until people pulled me off him."

"I understand why you did it."

"I shouldn't have. It didn't solve the issue. They were going to kick me out, and I was happy about it, but instead they forced me into counseling to work on my anger. In the end, it was the best thing that could have happened because I needed to talk to someone, and my therapist got through to me. I'd probably be a royally messed up adult if it wasn't for him." I wipe at the tear that slips down her cheek.

"I'm sorry. I shouldn't cry, it was your life, not mine."

"Don't ever apologize for your feelings. Own them. That is one thing therapy taught me. I still have a hard time putting it into practice, but I try to remind myself not to ignore or disregard how I feel."

She smiles and throws herself into my arms, her cheek on my chest. "You're amazing. I hope you know that."

"You might not think that when I leave the toilet seat up."

She shakes her head, giggling, and I squeeze her tightly.

"Let's go get a coffee," I say, and she nods.

We walk down the block, grab a coffee, and do some shopping together until I ask to separate from her for half an hour so that I can purchase her a gift. We end up having lunch after that, and the melancholy mood lifts to laughter and jokes.

She says I'm amazing, but she's the one who allows me to be fully transparent with my feelings. That means the world to me.

Chapter Twenty-Eight

BRYNN

We all sit around the table. I'm not even going to ask where Carter found these candy cane ice sculptures that sit between each couple.

"Only you," Tre says, staring at the twenty-four-inch ice block in front of him.

"And why exactly is the candy cane upside down?" Pierce asks.

I love that he's becoming more comfortable with my family.

"So it would stay standing up under the weight of the ice. You guys are the ones with dirty minds, I just want to make that clear." Carter looks between each one of us.

"All right, everyone. Hands and mouths only." Mom rolls her eyes. "Go!"

Pierce leans in. "I'll use my mouth on the lower part, and you use your hands. We'll swap when you get too cold."

"Okay." I bust out laughing, seeing Kenzie watching in amazement at Andrew licking the stick of the candy cane.

Pierce bends down and sucks the tip while I run my hands

up and down the main stick. Water drips down my wrists onto my forearms.

Tre's staring at us all as though he's about to tap out and not care about the win.

"You've got a good mouth, put it to use," Tessa tells him.

I swear I almost throw up a little in my mouth.

I don't even look my parents' way. Actually, that's a great idea. To get this done, I need to not look at my family members. One last glance down the table, and I see why Carter brought Faith on this trip. She's got the kind of skills that make me think she should be teaching a class.

Pierce's mouth pops off the ice before he goes back to sucking it like a giant ice cube that's attached to a pole or something. He watches my hands, his eyelids growing heavy. "On second thought. Let's switch."

I laugh, and he spins the sculpture around. I suck and lick while his hands slide up and down the shaft. There's no way we can do this and not have it seem sexual.

"I think you might have to let me take this one," Pierce whispers. "Because I'm going to embarrass myself if I have to watch you suck or stroke the candy cane any longer."

"You can thank me later," Carter says, not doing anything but watching Faith do all the work.

"Why don't you put those mediocre skills to the test?" I point at his ice sculpture.

Carter narrows his eyes. "Fine, I'll win this challenge."

"It's a stupid challenge, and we're getting rid of the rule that allowed it in the first place." Tre looks at Mom, and she nods.

Ew... ew... I need to stop looking around the table.

"This is really painful," Pierce says.

I slide my hand under the table to his crotch, and sure enough, he's hard from watching me suck on this ice stick as if it's his dick.

We have three wins, and Tre's not doing much. Carter is in go mode since I insulted his skills. I don't think we even need to do this challenge to secure the win.

"We're out," I say and cross my arms.

Tre quirks an eyebrow, but their sculpture is mostly just melting from being out of the freezer. Carter is about halfway done—mostly thanks to Faith's effort.

The other two teams aren't going to win the competition anyway.

"I'll let you pick the event," I say to Tre and put out my hand.

"Deal." He slides his hand into mine. "We're out."

"You can't do that!" Carter looks between us.

"Can and did." I stand. "Pierce and I have to do some wrapping. See you all at dinner."

Pierce doesn't waste any time walking out with me, then we're speed-walking toward our villa.

Once we're behind closed doors, I push him against the wall and palm the bulge in his pants. "It gets you all hot to see me sucking on something, huh?"

"You have no fucking idea. And thank you for your genius idea of getting us out of there."

I sink to my knees, not bothering to take off our boots, and wrap my fingers around the waist of his jeans.

"You look good on your knees," he says, palm cradling my cheek.

"Well, you look good enough to lick." I flick the button of his pants. He moans, and I slide down the zipper, tugging his jeans until they're at his knees. Then I take him out of his boxer briefs and fist his base, bringing the tip to my lips. "Should I tease you like you did me?"

"I think the ice sculpture was teasing enough." His hands grip my ponytail. I love the tug he gives it.

I slowly lick the side of his cock, then twirl the tip around my mouth.

"Jesus, your mouth." The back of his head hits the wall.

Yeah, there's nothing better than hearing that and taking the guy you're falling for to the edge, knowing it's all because of you.

And it's nice that Pierce is the reciprocating kind, because after he comes down my throat, he splays me out on the bed and returns the favor.

* * *

We're getting ready for dinner, though I really want to stay here with him and see how many positions we can master.

Pierce graciously allowed me to get ready first, so I'm on the couch with my laptop out, looking at The Mad Batter's current branding like Tessa asked me to. It's a cute bakery with an *Alice in Wonderland* theme. She's got cookies with phrases like Eat Me on them, which I love, but there's definitely some work and updating that could be done.

Pierce swings his legs behind me and sandwiches me between him and the computer, resting his chin on my shoulder. "What are you doing?"

"Looking at Tessa's bakery."

He doesn't say anything.

"What do you think?"

He kisses my neck. "I think you got this."

"Thank you, but I want to know what you see."

He sighs. "It's outdated. I'd probably overhaul the store, make a new logo that doesn't have *Alice in Wonderland* as a part of it. The shop name already implies it, and as long as she has goods to fulfill that demand for avid fans, she should expand to get people who couldn't care less about *Alice in Wonderland*."

"I was thinking the same thing. Plus, they're a small woman-owned business."

"All good things when it comes to consumers," he says.

"Look at the cute cookies." I point out the Eat Me cookies.

"I'll eat you." He pretends he's going to eat my neck, and I giggle.

"Hey." I close my laptop and turn around so I'm facing him. "We have a problem."

His forehead wrinkles. "What's the problem?"

I tilt my head. "We're up for the same job, remember?"

His head rocks back, and he smiles.

"Plus, we live in different countries."

"Not if I get the job over you." He winks then rests his forehead against mine. "Just kidding."

"I only ask because Christmas is in two days, then we're leaving here. I'm going back to Portland and…"

"I can go to Portland," he says as though it's no big deal.

"You mean until you hear from Enzo?"

Pierce sighs. "Honestly, I don't know what to do about that job. I'm really happy right now. I know we have to figure a lot out, but there's nothing for me in London."

My heart races. What is he saying?

"But there is a possibility of a job in New York. What if one of us gets that? What happens to the other one then? Or what if neither of us get it?" I ask.

I'm not even sure I want to live in New York City. It wasn't really my thing, but maybe Christmas is busier and crazier than usual. I should probably ask Tessa, since she lived there and moved to Portland with Tre after they met.

He shrugs. "If you get the job, I'm sure I can search for other marketing jobs in New York."

He can't really be already deciding that we go where the other goes.

"So, we try to stay in the same city?"

He runs his fingers down my back. "I'd like to. Is that not something you want? Would it be moving too fast?"

I think about it for a second. "Is it weird if it doesn't feel fast?"

He chuckles and kisses my cheek. "No. It's our decision on what we want to do. I don't want to be apart from you. I'm not asking for marriage or even living together, but I want to be in the same zip code. That's all."

I flip around and straddle his lap, clinging to him like a koala bear. "Me too. I want that too."

"Then let's do it. I'll go back to Portland with you until we hear back from Enzo, then we can make our decision on what to do. I'll even stay at a hotel, so you don't have to house me."

I rear back and look into his big green eyes. "You're staying with me, end of discussion. And can I just say how adult I feel right now? Like we've really got our shit together this time."

He laughs, and I cast kisses all over his beautiful face.

Life is good.

But Pierce is better.

Chapter Twenty-Nine

PIERCE

Ever since Brynn and I got together, time just flies by. It's Christmas Eve, and we spent the day on the slopes after she convinced me to rent a snowboard. Is there anything I wouldn't do for her? But it ended up being fun. Tre, Tessa, Kenzie, and Andrew all met us there. We spent a good part of the day on the mountain and thankfully didn't run into Kacey when we grabbed lunch. Then we came back for a nap. No surprise, Brynn and I didn't take a nap.

Now it's time to head over to the main house to have dinner with everyone.

Gwen and Abe are already in the kitchen when we arrive, so I go over to help them.

"What can I do?" I ask.

"Nothing, go enjoy your holiday. You've helped enough this week." Gwen nudges me to leave, but it doesn't seem right to allow them to do all the cooking on their own.

I laugh and am ready to turn around when I spot something on the mantel.

All week, the stockings have hung above the fireplace, and I haven't really thought much of them. They're clearly all handmade. Each one has a Santa or a snowman or a reindeer with each person's name stitched across it.

Now there's a new one right next to Brynn's.

A hand lands on my forearm. "I didn't know if I'd have it done on time. But I finished it this morning." Gwen smiles.

"But... I'm not..." The words refuse to come out.

"Oh, Pierce, I knew it the minute you admitted to knowing Brynn before you arrived here. The way she looked at you, a mother knows. And even if you two don't work out, for some reason that is beyond me, you're one of us now. But if Faith asks, say that Brynn made it for you. I don't want her to feel bad, but you know..."

She squeezes my arm and walks away before I can say thank you.

Brynn walks up to me, trailing her fingers down my chest like I love. "Why are you so white?"

"Your mum made me a stocking." I'm still staring at my name stitched across the top, hung with everyone else's, as if I'm a part of the family. My gut twists, and my chest tightens.

"I know." Brynn smiles wide. "She was so happy she was able to finish it in time and thankful when she bought the kit for Kenzie's family that it came with four." Brynn turns around and admires the stocking. "We look good next to one another."

I can't speak. The words aren't coming out. I stand there silently, like an idiot, for a moment before I'm able to finally push some words past my lips. "Excuse me."

I kiss the top of Brynn's head and walk out the back door by the fire pit. I stand by the fire, watching the orange flames and feeling the warmth, my heart still beating out of my chest no matter what I try to do to calm it down.

The door opens behind me, and I expect it to be Andrew, but when arms wrap around my waist, I know it's Brynn.

"Are you okay?"

I place my hand over hers where it rests on my stomach. "I will be. Just give me a minute."

"Okay." She walks around me and sits in one of the chairs, crossing her legs and staring into the fire.

"You can go inside," I say, unable to look her in the eye. "It's cold out here."

"I know I can, but I won't."

"Brynn..."

She sits up and rests her elbows on her knees. "I get that something is going on, but I'm not leaving this chair. Take all the time you need, but I'm not going inside without you. If you want to talk it out, I'm here. If you don't want to talk, consider me your silent support committee."

I inhale a deep breath and blow out an even bigger one. "I'm really fighting the instinct to withdraw and leave." I walk around the fire and take the chair next to her. "It's scary to me. I've never felt a part of a family like this, and throughout the week, I've grown really close with yours. To see a symbol of family and be included in it... and for your mum to work on it all week... it brings up a lot of stuff for me. It means I'm cared for, but also that I care for them. And it's hard for me to untangle family from heartbreak. I know what it feels like to lose people you feel like that about, and I don't want to go through it again."

Tears glisten in Brynn's eyes. "I understand."

I take her hands, warming them with mine. "Don't get me wrong, it's the nicest thing anyone's done for me, and I appreciate it. I just needed to pull myself together and remind myself not to run. Not to pull back, but to embrace it."

She stands and sits on my lap, hugging me. "Can I have that therapist's number?"

I chuckle and draw back. "If not for the work he told me to do, I never would have been able to go back inside and welcome the unconditional love your family gives."

"We can sit out here all night," she says, relaxing into my chest.

I lean back, hugging her into my body and enjoying the peace I feel with her that finally calms my beating heart.

Before long, Tre and Tessa come out with Ryah. And then Andrew and Kenzie with Nolan. The party migrates outside before I ever have to go back in, and it feels better than I would have thought to have people have my back. People who want to be around me. People I can rely on, and they can rely on me. It feels like being a part of a family again, and I realize that I wouldn't trade it for anything, no matter how hard it is to accept.

Chapter Thirty

PIERCE

On Christmas morning, I sneak out of bed and place Brynn's gifts under our *Elf* tree, then tiptoe back into bed.

Even though it's Christmas, we decided last night that since the kids are so young and don't know what day it is, we'll all sleep in and make brunch and open presents later this morning. Maybe it's odd to be spending the holiday with a family I didn't know until this past week, but they've been so open and welcoming that it doesn't feel weird.

"I heard you, you know," Brynn says as I crawl under the covers and spoon her.

"Merry Christmas." I kiss the nape of her neck. "Do you want your present?"

"I feel your present." She wiggles her ass into my hardened dick.

"That present can wait until after you open your real gift."

She shakes her head and rolls over to face me. "It feels pretty real to me."

I chuckle and kiss her lips. "Come on."

"You're antsy this morning." She pushes her body against

mine, swarming me with her arms and legs. "Let's just stay in bed all day."

"Well, your parents might be upset, and you want to see Ryah open her gift from you, right?"

Brynn throws her head back on an exasperated groan. "Why do you always have to be so sensible?" She rolls back over and swings her legs over the edge of the bed, still scouring the floor just in case our pet mouse comes back. "Let me brush my teeth."

I watch her naked body walk to the bathroom and hear the water running a second later. I feel as if my Christmas wish has already come true.

She comes out a few minutes later, and I lead her to the couch. I already moved her two gifts to the coffee table.

"Two! We said one," she says, pouting.

"Don't worry. Just pick one and open it." She reaches for one. "Not that one, the other one."

Laughing, she looks over her shoulder at me and picks up the other box. Careful not to rip the wrapping paper, she opens it and sees the white box. I hope she's not expecting jewelry because I'd hate to disappoint her on our first holiday.

"Lift the lid." I'm way too eager for her to see what it is.

"I will," she says, her hand wrapping around the white box, lifting the lid to reveal her present. "Pierce. Are you sure you want to part with this?" She holds up the *I Heart London* keychain. "I love it." She leans forward and kisses me.

"I wish I could have put a key to my place on it, but the only place I have is my flat in London. So, as soon as I find a place wherever we land, you're getting a key to my place."

She laughs and leans her head on my shoulder. "It means a lot. Thank you."

"Next." I nod toward the other present.

"Where is the Pierce I know? You're so excited, and you said you were pretty blah about Christmas."

"That was before I got you." I swing my body so I'm behind her, my arms under hers and my legs stretched around her body.

She picks up the next gift, being just as gentle with the wrapping paper.

"Just rip it."

She does and finds another box, so she lifts the lid and removes the tissue paper.

"Ohhh..." She picks up the "Our First Christmas" ornament that has mistletoe painted on it.

"I figure we can collect one each year. The mistletoe represents the moment when I finally felt like we might have a future together. I'll never forget that kiss under the mistletoe in front of the fire."

She circles around and sits on her ankles, hugging me. "I can't believe I gave you the cold shoulder. Thank you for both gifts, I love them." She turns and gets up off the couch to put the ornament on the tree. "Perfect." Then she turns to look at me. "I'll be right back."

She heads down the hall to the bathroom, and I hear her rooting around in the cupboard under the sink.

Brynn comes back with a package, and sitting down beside me, she places it in my hands. "I hope you like it."

"I'm sure I'll like it."

It's been years since I've gotten a Christmas gift—unless it was from another professor, and those were mostly exchanges of some sort. I never exchanged gifts with Andrew or his parents or any of the other relatives once I was an adult.

I run my finger under the wrapping paper and the tape pops off.

"Rip it," she says like I told her.

"Looks like someone else is eager to have their present opened too."

She eyes the gift, and I finish unwrapping it. It's in a

brown box and has some weight to it. There are no markings on the box.

When I open it and pick up the item, I have to choke back tears. "Brynn…"

"I really hope I didn't overstep, and if you don't like it, we can return it or throw it away. But I wanted you to have one." She bites her lip as tears fill her eyes.

I unwrap the tissue paper from around the snow globe of Utah. The slopes inside have little skiers and snowboarders.

"It's not the North Pole, but it's where we started over. I hope you can look at it and remember your mom and also think of our time this week. If you're up for it, we can carry on the tradition and buy snow globes every year."

I shake the globe and watch the snow whoosh around the dome, falling on the little skiers. "It's perfect. I really appreciate all the thought."

She takes the globe and shakes it. "They're kind of addictive. It took me forever to wrap it because I kept shaking it."

I hug her back to my front and kiss her shoulder. "Thank you for a wonderful Christmas."

"It's not over yet."

She swivels around, sets the globe on the coffee table, and stands, offering me her hand. I slide my palm in hers and rise to my feet, allowing her to lead me to the bed. Hell, I'd follow this woman anywhere.

Epilogue

BRYNN

We're at my apartment in Portland on New Year's Eve, cleaning up the dishes after the delicious meal that Pierce cooked.

He returned to Portland with me like he said, and we've been working on The Mad Batter's brand marketing all week —when we're not screwing like bunnies. But we've managed to visit both locations, which enabled him to see my small hometown of Climax Cove and meet all the locals. They kept asking him to say specific words over and over so they could hear his accent, and though I'm sure he hated it, he took it all in stride.

"I was thinking about something." I turn around to face him after I'm done filling the dishwasher.

"Yeah?" he asks, grabbing two champagne glasses and a bottle from the fridge.

"On Monday, I'm going to tell Enzo Mancini that I'm not interested in the job." I bite my lip. Taking myself out of the race for the position wasn't an easy decision. It's guaranteed income, and what I'm about to do is really scary.

"What? Why?" he asks, twisting the cork of the champagne bottle to open it.

"Because I want to go out on my own."

He lowers the bottle and raises his eyebrows. "Really?"

"I know it's crazy, and you probably think you're dating a nut. You won't have to support me if you're worried about that."

He laughs. "I'm not."

"But I don't know... I work for a firm now, and there are a lot of rules and policies, and it has to go through this person and that person for approval. Do you know how many ideas they turn down because they're afraid to try anything too different, then someone else ends up doing it, and it explodes with popularity? Maybe it's working on the bakery brand, I don't know. But I want to be the one to make the decisions. I know it will be a slow start, and I'm really scared, but I think it's the right decision for me."

He comes over and places his hands on my hips. "Breathe."

I inhale and exhale a few times. "It's just you're taking a huge chance with me and my family, and that got me thinking. Change doesn't come without fear, and rewards don't happen if you don't push the fear aside and just do it. I'd rather regret that it didn't work out than that I didn't try."

"It will work out," he says before pressing his lips to my forehead. "You can make anything turn to gold, but if it doesn't, I'll be here to support you."

"There's another thing." And this is the scariest part, but I told myself to do this before the clock strikes midnight. So here goes nothing.

"Okay?" He steps back to go to the table, but I tug him back to me.

"I want a partner." I bite my lip again.

"Do you have someone in mind? Someone you worked with at the firm here?"

I shake my head.

"Why do you think you need a partner?" He tilts his head and studies my face.

"I don't need one, I want one."

He chuckles. "If you don't know someone, you'll have to put an ad out and do some interviews, I guess." He shifts to walk away, and I tug him back. "Brynn?"

"I know someone." I swallow the lump in my throat.

"Okay, ask them then. If they say no, find someone else. But I really think you can do this on your own."

"Will you?"

He blinks, obviously trying to figure out where I'm going with this.

"Be my partner. It's insane, I know. I'm fully aware that embarking on this with you... you can say no. If you don't want to or think that would be too much, too soon for us, I get it."

He laughs and dips his head to my neck. "Have I ever told you I love it when you're nervous and ramble?"

My cheeks heat. "No."

"Well, I do. And have I ever told you that I'm pretty sure both of us are crazy, but I also know I've never felt this way about anyone. I know in my gut you are the one for me."

"And if not?" I ask.

"Good thing we're pretty good at the adulting thing. I think we'll be okay."

I cross my fingers just to be safe.

He presses his lips to my neck and trails kisses up to my ear. "I'd love to be your partner, Brynn Russell," he whispers.

I squeal and wind my arms around his neck. "Really?"

He shifts back to look at me. "Really."

"Oh... thank you."

"Thanks for asking." He kisses me again. "Now let's open the champagne."

We decided to celebrate New Year's Eve in the Eastern time zone with Andrew and Kenzie via video call, so Pierce is about to pop the bottle of champagne when the doorbell rings. I open the door to let my parents in. They walk in and kiss my cheek, saying hello and Happy New Year.

I close the door behind them.

Pierce greets them and pulls down two more glasses.

Another knock lands on the door, and I open it to find Tre and Tessa and Ryah.

Pierce pulls down two more glasses and fills one of Ryah's sippy cups she left here full of apple juice.

I move away from the door to join all our guests when Pierce's phone rings. It's Kenzie, Andrew, and Nolan on a video call.

The doorbell rings again, and I open the door to find Carter... alone.

"What are you doing—" I smile and pull him in for a hug, shocked that he's not in New York.

"Pierce invited me, and I had miles to turn in."

Pierce opens up another bottle of champagne and pours everyone a glass. Then he comes over to hand one to me.

I give him a questioning look. "What did you do?"

Everyone else sits in my small living area with their glasses of champagne, waiting for the ball to drop on the television.

"They say to spend New Year's Eve with the people you want to spend the year with. And I want to spend it with everyone in this room." Pierce nods toward everyone in the room. "Especially the woman standing to my right."

I grin at him. "She's not going anywhere."

"I hope not. Happy New Year, Brynn. One of many to come."

"One of many." I clink my glass to him, but we don't drink.

We walk toward the back of the couch as my family counts down, then we all yell "Happy New Year!" clink our glasses again, and take a sip.

My gaze shoots to Pierce talking with my brothers, then my mom and dad playing with Ryah. Tessa's talking to Andrew and Kenzie on the phone.

Family is everything, and I can't wait for Pierce to join mine *officially* someday.

The End

Also by Piper Rayne

Holiday Romances

Single and Ready to Jingle

Claus and Effect

Merry Kissmas

The Nest

Mr. Heartbreaker

Mr. Broody

Mr. S (Title to be revealed)

Mr. C (Title to be revealed)

Kingsmen Football Stars

False Start (Free Prequel)

You Had Your Chance, Lee Burrows

You Can't Kiss the Nanny, Brady Banks

Over My Brother's Dead Body, Chase Andrews

Chicago Grizzlies

On the Defense (Free Prequel)

Something like Hate

Something like Lust

Something like Love

Plain Daisy Ranch

One Last Summer

The One I Left Behind
The One I Stood Beside
The One I Didn't See Coming

The Baileys

Lessons from a One-Night Stand (FREE)
Advice from a Jilted Bride
Birth of a Baby Daddy
Operation Bailey Wedding (Novella)
Falling for My Brother's Best Friend
Demise of a Self-Centered Playboy
Confessions of a Naughty Nanny
Operation Bailey Babies (Novella)
Secrets of the World's Worst Matchmaker
Winning my Best Friend's Girl
Rules for Dating Your Ex
Operation Bailey Birthday (Novella)

The Greene Family

My Twist of Fortune (Free Prequel)
My Beautiful Neighbor (FREE)
My Almost Ex
My Vegas Groom
A Greene Family Summer Bash (Novella)
My Sister's Flirty Friend
My Unexpected Surprise
My Famous Frenemy
A Greene Family Vacation (Novella)

My Scorned Best Friend

My Fake Fiancé

My Brother's Forbidden Friend

A Greene Family Christmas (Novella)

Lake Starlight

The Problem with Second Chances

The Issue with Bad Boy Roommates

The Trouble with Runaway Brides

The Drawback of Single Dads

Modern Love

Charmed by the Bartender

Hooked by the Boxer

Mad about the Banker

Single Dads Club

Real Deal

Dirty Talker

Sexy Beast

Hollywood Hearts

Mister Mom

Animal Attraction

Domestic Bliss

Bedroom Games

Cold as Ice

On Thin Ice

Break the Ice

Cockamamie Unicorn Ramblings

Happy Holidays! We hope you loved our quick and cute second chance love story between Brynn and Pierce.

When we first started writing the holiday books it was to bring a standalone in our offering of books for people who don't love to read a series, but I think it's safe to say at this point, we're just series writers. Single and Ready to Jingle (Kenzie and Andrew's story) was going to be a one off, but of course we spun Tessa out for Claus and Effect because we're us. Then we kept finding a throughline in the reviews of Claus and Effect—readers wanted Brynn's story. And of course they did! Because we're all romance readers and we want everyone to get their happily ever after! LOL

Pierce wasn't always going to be British, but we really wanted to use Shane East as a narrator, so we originally intended for Pierce to be Andrew's brother, until we went back and read Single and Ready to Jingle and realized he didn't have a sibling (it's comical really). We also thought we'd center the mountain town gathering around Tessa and Tre's wedding, until we realized they were already married in the epilogue of Claus and Effect. Are you sensing a theme here? LOL With the wedding idea out, we threw a lot of other ideas out there which brought us to a second chance romance, always one of our faves. Once that was decided, we had to figure out how if Pierce lived in London and Brynn lived in Portland, where in the world did, they originally meet to make this a second chance? Logistics. Always a writer's nemesis. But we both loved the idea of writing a weekend fling that turned into a missed opportunity. There's something magical about having an instant connection with someone, but to have it not work out left us ripe with possibilities.

The best thing about writing this book was the family dynamic. The banter between siblings, the new additions welcomed with open arms, and the two little babies were what we loved most about this book.

Honestly, there were probably a lot of things that we changed that we can't remember. This one seemed to be a story that kept evolving and morphing until we reach the end!

As always, we have a lot of people to thank for getting this book into your hands!

Nina and the entire Valentine PR team.

Cassie from Joy Editing for line edits. Thank you for being so accommodating with the deadline for this one.

My Brother's Editor for line edits and proofreading.

Hang Le for the cover and branding it to match Single and Ready to Jingle and Claus and Effect.

All the bloggers who read, review, share and/or promote us.

The Piper Rayne Unicorns in our Facebook group who are always our biggest cheerleaders!

Every reader who took the time to read this book! Thank you for granting us your most precious resource—time. We don't take that lightly.

If you haven't already read Single and Ready to Jingle or Claus and Effect, we encourage you to check them out for a little more holiday love and to see how Andrew and Kenzie and Tre and Tessa got their happy ever afters!

We hope you have a wonderful holiday season and new year!

xo,
Piper & Rayne

About Piper & Rayne

Piper Rayne is a *USA Today* Bestselling Author duo who write "heartwarming humor with a side of sizzle" about families, whether that be blood or found. They both have e-readers full of one-clickable books, they're married to husbands who drive them to drink, and they're both chauffeurs to their kids. Most of all, they love hot heroes and quirky heroines who make them laugh, and they hope you do, too!

Printed in Great Britain
by Amazon